visigoth

visi

GARY AMDAHL

goth

stories

MILKWEED EDITIONS

Published 2006 by Milkweed Editions
Printed in Canada
Cover design by Christian Fuenfhausen
Cover photo © Grigory Dukor/Corbis
Interior design and typesetting by Percolator
The text of this book is set in Zingha.
06 07 08 09 10 5 4 3 2 1
First Edition

Milkweed Editions, a nonprofit publisher, gratefully acknowledges sustaining support from Emilie and Henry Buchwald; Bush Foundation; Patrick and Aimee Butler Family Foundation; Cargill Value Investment; Timothy and Tara Clark Family Charitable Fund; Dougherty Family Foundation; Ecolab Foundation; General Mills Foundation; Greystone Foundation; Institute for Scholarship in the Liberal Arts, College of Arts and Sciences, University of Notre Dame; Constance B. Kunin; Marshall Field's Gives; McKnight Foundation; a grant from the Minnesota State Arts Board, through an appropriation by the Minnesota State Legislature, a grant from the National Endowment for the Arts, and private funders; an award from the National Endowment for the Arts, which believes that a great nation deserves great art; Navarre Corporation; Debbie Reynolds; St. Paul Travelers Foundation; Ellen and Sheldon Sturgis; Target Foundation; Gertrude Sexton Thompson Charitable Trust (George R. A. Johnson, Trustee); James R. Thorpe Foundation; Toro Foundation; Serene and Christopher Warren; W. M. Foundation; and Xcel Energy Foundation.

Library of Congress Cataloging-in-Publication Data

Amdahl, Gary, 1956–
Visigoth / Gary Amdahl.—1st ed.
p. cm.
ISBN-13: 978-1-57131-051-4 (pbk. : acid-free paper)
ISBN-10: 1-57131-051-7 (pbk. : acid-free paper)
I. Title.
PS3601.M38V57 2006
813'.6—dc22
2005027264

This book is printed on acid-free paper.

40th ANNIVERSARY

NATIONAL
ENDOWMENT
FOR THE ARTS
Established 1965

MINNESOTA
STATE ARTS BOARD

For Leslie

visigoth

He exalted his lusts. He ferreted out odd acts of violence that he had committed and forgotten about. The whole conception of transferring guilt, which once had seemed desirable, became repulsive when offered as salvation.
—PATRICK WHITE, THE TREE OF MAN

"It turned out that I don't write in order to seek pleasure; on the contrary, it turned out that by writing I am seeking pain, the most acute possible, well-nigh intolerable pain, most likely because pain is truth, and as to what constitutes truth, I wrote, the answer is so simple: truth is what consumes you, I wrote."
—IMRE KERTÉSZ, KADDISH FOR AN UNBORN CHILD

"Above all things, let no unwary reader do me the injustice of believing in me. In that I write at all I am among the damned. If he must believe in anything, let him believe in the music of Handel, the painting of Giovanni Bellini, and in the thirteenth chapter of St. Paul's First Epistle to the Corinthians."
—SAMUEL BUTLER, NOTE-BOOKS 1874-1902

visigoth

the
flyweight

Dennis Hurt was perhaps not classically handsome. He looked, we sometimes kidded him, like a tiny Frankenstein's Monster: pale, five-two, veins like dark throbbing ropes tangled about his arms and neck, bicepses like surgically implanted softballs. Beginning to gray already at eighteen, his dark brows nearly met in the middle and there were deep purple half-moons beneath remarkably large and impenetrable black eyes.

His brothers were significantly younger than Dennis, and significantly taller as well. His father was tall, too, a slender man whom Dennis liked to say he could bust up like a pretzel rod. He said so not with animosity, because he loved his father and his beanpole brothers like crazy, but merely to point out how strange fathers and sons can be to each other—families too. And to suggest, on a sort

of philosophical note, that there ought not be such dis-
parities of power between people.

His father, who worked the long, private hours of a
melancholy and inward man leading a public and successful life, was the senior pastor of a very large Lutheran
church—the biggest in the world, it was widely believed.
At the same time, however, he was a drop-dead business-
man, a crackerjack venture capitalist, exceptionally astute
regarding his portfolio, and a good landlord. Pastor Hurt
chaired the Christian Business Fellowship Network, and
had just performed—at the time I am writing of, which
is many years ago now—a narrow escape from a deal he
knew in hindsight he should not have even heard about.
There was this entrepreneur, nominally Christian, who
had obtained funds to buy some medical equipment from
a company in dire straits, with the idea that he would
lease the equipment back to the company, but what he
did was just hand the money over to the CEO, which, if I
understood correctly, constituted fraud. There was transport of something over a state line and some other magic
tricks, and exactly where Pastor Hurt fit in, I'm not sure.
Both Dennis and I got lost in that kind of conversation
quite easily, so I just can't say.

Dennis's mother left his father because there wasn't
enough of him to go around. At the time it was also useful
as an illustration of how pastors are just people too. As
far as Dennis went, he simply felt there was no point of
contact between his father and himself. They had almost
nothing in common: a shoe size that was some tremendous
figure I never actually pinned down, a preference for black

industrial-style crepe-soled shoes, big hands with long slender piano-player fingers. But where Dennis was rippling with muscle everywhere on his little frame, his father's limbs were weak-looking and skinny, legs for instance riding straight up into his back, no rear end to speak of, loose and worn khaki trousers flapping about his bones. He wore big square glasses in thick black frames—Dennis could read a printed page across the room—and a small, dirty-looking moustache that I felt did his sincere face a terrible disservice. I don't think Dennis characterized him as a pretzel rod because he was physically so much weaker—he was in fact quite strong—but because they were so different, so mysteriously, agonizingly different.

Dennis and I were on the wrestling team. I wasn't particularly good, but Dennis had never been defeated. Not once in four years. Our coach once said to some people gathered to honor him that you could not buy what Dennis had. He meant it in the usual complimentary way, but up there on the dais with his dinner untouched, Dennis was struck with fear: oh my god, he thought, what do I have, what do I have, oh my god. "What he had" had troubled him since he first suspected he had it; to hear it announced in a ballroom was alarming. Coach went on to describe it as stick-to-itiveness and the ability, the will, to give a hundred and seventeen percent whenever anyone asked for it. I think that's what he said. He was a nubbin-headed old boar hog for whom nobody had the least respect, but he and Dennis were kind of in business together—and this relationship was terribly important to Dennis. Once when

Coach was obviously in his cups, maudlin as could be, he admitted he was just pissing in the wind. Dennis was a once-in-a-lifetime wrestler who would win a gold medal and a seat in Congress and he wanted to help. "*How can I help you?*" he cried.

He used my friend to teach younger wrestlers, took him all over the place, establishing himself as the mentor, hanging a plumb bob from the front strap of Denny's headgear and having him walk over desks and things to illustrate the proper relation of head and knees. They shot a training film together called *Wrestling for Champions*. These are the seven fundamentals, Coach croaks in voice-overs and gruesome head shots. Posture: there Denny is with the plumb bob. Motion: he stutter-steps left and right, forward and backward, like some jumped-up crab. Changing Levels: he does a kind of limbo-stick drill. Penetration: the Giant Stride Into Your Opponent (which is me). Lifting: he hoists a few teammates (again I am in the picture looking stupid). Backstep: a Greco-Roman two-hundred-seventy-degree spin-and-throw. Finally, the Back Arch: back to a gym wall, Dennis bends over backward until his palms are against the wall, then walks himself up and down it. For the dramatic fun of it, he feigns a grapple with Coach, who outweighs him by a couple hundred pounds, and falls over backward with Coach atop him. But just when you think he has been crushed to death, you see Coach go flying into the camera with a miked-up crash. A little later, after the arm-bars and nelsons both full and half and head-levers and cradles, he's talking about strategies: your strong wrestler likes to work in close and your quick

wrestler likes room to move. The first will crowd you
and the second surprise you. But the best wrestler—cut
to Dennis in competition—is both quick and strong: you
crowd this guy, thinking you're stronger, and he'll embroil
you in his power, but if you try to work from a distance,
thinking you're faster, he'll run you ragged—cut to shot of
ref holding Denny's arm up. He looked bored, but I knew
he was anything but.

One morning, toward the middle of Denny's fourth season
of seamless victory, we stood at our narrow beige lockers, working the tumblers, when Linda the pom-pom girl
arrived, shooting glances I couldn't begin to describe or
understand—everything to everybody—and kissed Dennis
on the cheek.

Linda came from good Christian stock as well. Her
feeling—which she asserted not merely as Christian but
as practical—was that we were living the best years of our
lives. Dennis and I slumped against our lockers, taking in
the milling and listening to Linda as she fell into an ad-
monitory, then a motherly, tone: best years of our lives.

Dennis said, "I can't believe that."

Linda gaped, I smiled.

"We will look back on these years," said Linda, "these
yuh—"

"*No we won't,*" Denny said sternly, "and do you know
why? Because these years *suck the dick of the Great Woolly
Mammoth,* that's why."

"What is the matter with you, anyway?" Linda's pom-
poms rustled in agitation, then fell silently to her side.

Being, after all, not truly comfortable with colorful language like that, Dennis shrugged and said, "Long thought to be extinct."

"You're hallucinating," said Linda, "right now, aren't you? Why don't you eat something instead of grossing out people who only want to help you adjust to normal life?"

It was true that he was fasting. He fasted recklessly, religiously, not so much to stay under a hundred pounds, but rather to maintain in himself that sense that he was both a good dog, doing his duty, and a computer, binary, no options, win or lose. Too much food and he started feeling sassy, preternatural. The graphed X and Y of energy and weight rose and fell respectively, met at the optimal point, then shot sharply off the chart in two directions. Dennis associated "emaciated" with "meek" and thought he would continue to inherit the earth either way.

Linda flounced off with a shout of good cheer and Dennis looked down at his legs, which were deeply bowed, as if in shame. A very tall boy, taller than anybody in the school, a boy we knew only by sight, came up and stood so close to us that Dennis had to drop his head back on his shoulders to take him in. He was not fat, but certainly heavy with loose meat all over him. He smiled like he was excited to be near us, and spoke with a faint southern accent and a mild stutter. There was a long, soft, almost sweet "Howwww," and then an up-tempo "much can you bench-press?" He dropped his head on his chest to look at Dennis. I asked him how much he tipped the scales at, and the tall boy came back with a figure more than double Denny's. "He could press you, Man Mountain!" I said. The tall boy laughed hysterically, then wiped his mouth and apologized. He tugged from his pants pockets five one-dollar bills, whereupon we trooped down to the weight room and I took his money as Dennis cleaned and jerked the tall boy's weight. I said, "Tell your friends what you saw here." Other performances included one-handed pull-ups and benching one hundred pounds on the Universal Gym for five minutes without a significant break in rhythm.

I managed these affairs. Dennis and I were best friends. I would like to think we still are friends. But whatever is between us now, he thought very highly of me then. I was, he said too many times, the Renaissance man, pulling him and Linda both through chemistry and physics in my wake, singing the part of Nathan Detroit in the school play, explaining to him the difference between wet black deposits on the spark plugs of our motorcycles, and dry black deposits. I played the trumpet and the guitar and the piano, he told everybody within earshot. He believed I was extremely successful with women, shouting jokes at them in the incredulous manner of an acerbic stand-up comic, then just kind of becoming one with them, never making an overt move or pass, enveloping them somehow, while they huffed and puffed all over me with ardor. I was a three-letter man, and if I wasn't the world's greatest wrestler, so what?

I was indeed a mediocre wrestler. I lost so many times it made Dennis uneasy in the bowels to spectate. Though I was nearly a foot taller than him, with seventy more pounds, he rode me easily around the mat, using the basic moves and holds and often waving a free arm like a bronc rider. It's easy to imagine me hating him for such showboating. But it's also easy, I think, for the reader to imagine him hating me—or maybe envying me and being ashamed of himself, watching me slip with unerring instinct from girl of his dreams to girl of his dreams. Hate is too strong a word. I do not think friends can hate each other. But certainly we had a friendship referring dangerously to sex and violence and little else. But what else is there? That is in fact the question Dennis put to the Christ when He came to him in the vision.

Dennis could feel something like a tendon parting inside his head that winter. He was emaciated as usual but miraculously stronger than ever. The good dog in him was thinking more and more of Jesus, seeing that shape in Eternity and adding it to the unswerving sense of duty. But he struggled with it, more or less like any son of a pastor would. The computer continued to churn bits. He felt something very like a membrane start to tear, felt a burning along that line, right down the middle. In an instinctive bid to acknowledge and banish it in one fell swoop, he dramatized it. (He'd just seen *Guys and Dolls*, and really thought I was onto something. The thrill and glory of athletic endeavor is there, on stage, but it's not nearly so lonely. Everybody loves everybody else, even when—especially when—they appear to hate and wish to conquer or upstage each other!)

We went to the gym and started climbing rope. This was something we did every other day: thirty feet, unknotted, up and down ten times. It was rugged exercise for me, but Dennis didn't even use his legs. It was cold that day on the dark, varnished floor, but warm up at the top where the high windows let in long boxes of dusty light. I finished five and took a rest. Dennis stopped up at the top and dangled, listening to that slow split of membrane.

"Lance," he said in a little voice, the voice of a baby angel floating up there, "I think I'm losing my grip."

And let go of the rope with one hand.

He turned slowly in a full circle, then back the other way. I exclaimed my appreciation: it was something I had not seen before, something, certainly, to add to the show.

Then he monkeyed down the rope, actually jabbering, let go with both hands and bounced hard on the gleaming floor, leapt back up and rocketed to the top, hand over blurred hand, feet dangling motionless as if he were riding an invisible elevator or was crippled, the end of the rope quivering only slightly he was so smooth, up and down, up and down, like he was crazy, dropping from higher and higher up the rope, slamming into the floor and firing back up in smooth, relentless, furious ascent and descent. He finished and said he felt like ripping somebody's limbs off and sobbing for a week. He chuckled when he said this, encouraging me to do likewise. We stood there, heaving, glaring, snickering. Turned out he was stoned. This, too, was a first for us. His snickering imperturbability and comic indifference to the real danger his extreme condition put him in was like flypaper to me. I admired him much more deeply and confusedly than I could say.

The days grew clamorous as Dennis sojourned from victory to victory and the likelihood of a fourth consecutive state championship grew and grew. One morning, a TV crew idled their van in front of Dennis's house, talking to Coach and waiting for him and Dennis to walk out the door as they'd planned. Dennis burst through the door and began running as fast as he could. The van chirped its tires, a sound that echoed up and down the quiet street. He stopped abruptly after only a mile, completely winded it seemed, and the driver of the van slammed on the brakes. The cameraman and the reporter threw open their respective doors and got out. "How does it feel?" the reporter asked. "Three times state champ, four seasons without a single defeat. Doesn't that make you feel, you know, a little nervous? How do you feel on the eve of—?"

"I *feel*," Dennis said with startling truculence, "like I can take *care* of myself."

They wanted to share more of his day, so we jogged another couple miles, slowly, allowing the cameraman to jog with us, for effect. At school we ushered them into the dark gym and reeled a little hemp. He went up and came down a few times and then a whirlwind of his actual, secret fears and anxieties engulfed him. Dangling in the warm dusty box, he quoted some fabulous Psalms of David at the crew, about the eyes of his enemies standing out with fatness and how he would break the teeth of them all, pour their brains out like the viscera of pigs. He let go of the rope with one hand, then the other. By the time he refastened, he was moving downward at a great clip. The rope sliced deeply into his hands; it was like grabbing a spinning drill bit. When he got to the bottom, he held them out for inspection: they were burned white. As we stared, thin seams and spots of blood appeared on his palms. Then suddenly they were awash. The crew recorded this in professional silence. As they were leaving, the reporter said, "We're into spectacular pictures, you know, in our biz, people being plucked from raging rivers and so on, but I don't think this is something we can use. It's just too strange. But it'll be in our tape library if you ever, you know, want to check back."

The station's news director, however, had other ideas, and broadcast the footage. The gist of the segment was that Dennis had miscalculated and was now wounded. It was the talk of the meet. Nobody paid the least bit of attention to all the great wrestling going on—they were all waiting to see if he would do something wicked, crazy, or foolish. It was a given he would attempt one of the three, and then the question was, would he be punished for it and fail, or would he be punished for it and prevail? Everybody wanted him to be, or assumed he would be, punished in some way. The idea that it would be a walk for him—as every other match had been for years—was dismissed.

Did he win? He grew quite manic and fierce as he advanced from one round to the next, eyes blazing, immobile and mute outside the ring, remorseless and cruel inside it. He actually threw one hapless contender out of the circle and knocked the ref over with him. It was so humiliating he just stood there shaking his head, which everybody seemed to think was a sign of contempt and more or less admirable, given the culture of sports spectatorship, and yes, I think it was contempt at first, but it was changing even as he stood there, becoming sorrow and fear before he was off the mat.

But whatever it was, nobody had seen anything like it, and there were pictures of him in all three of the metropolitan area newspapers, in the community weeklies as well, his neck looking grotesquely wide, the ribbons of his medal angling away from each other out of the frame, brow dark and humorless, eyes black and dead, bottom lip protruding slightly as if he were pouting over his supremacy. (He'd taken a clout from a flailing, panic-stricken worm.) It was a ghastly piece of comic portraiture, but everybody who saw it saw the Dennis they thought they knew: goofy, lurking, rangy, confused. *Sports Illustrated* used the shot for "Faces in the Crowd." A guy from the Greco-Roman set tried to woo him with tales of Olympic gold, as did a rep of the sweet science. He told them the summer was going to be devoted to soul-searching, relaxation—even a bit of partying—and competitive weight lifting (because he was tired of hurting people, he confided in me only).

Even though nearly a decade had passed from the Summer of Love to that summer, we all still listened to *Sgt. Pepper's Lonely Hearts Club Band*. Dennis got the hang of both pot—smoking it indiscreetly all summer long, at parties and even in public—and sexual intercourse. He witnessed ardently for both Jesus Christ and free love, and nobody saw a conflict, save maybe Linda, who wanted him for herself. We heard the nascent Christianity in Van Morrison and indulged in the astringent irony of Steely Dan just to feel sophisticated, freely interpreting their obscure lyrics to suit ourselves.

I found myself increasingly in another camp. The parties I favored featured people we didn't know, drugs we hadn't heard of, and sex and violence on a scale I hadn't thought possible. Sometimes Dennis came with me and held his own, and sometimes, feeling guilty, did not.

At the last party of the summer, things went predictably from really good to really bad. At first Dennis couldn't remember anybody's name, not Linda's, not mine—nobody's. Befuddlement, grinning befuddlement, in such an environment, was easily dismissed. In fact it was hardly noticed. But whatever was actually happening to him was being confused in his mind with the once-serious and still lingering idea that he had never suffered defeat and that therefore everybody in the room had met anonymous doom at his hands. Alarmingly soon after the names disappeared, he began to lose faces too. This, too, of course, can happen to anybody, especially when you move even just slightly out of your circle: of course faces are going to seem strange, and the more you've isolated or insulated your brain, peninsulated it, the stranger and more menacing they will seem. Nobody, at any rate that night, looked quite familiar enough, somehow, for Dennis to talk to. Everything moved more quickly than he thought it should. The minute hand on his wristwatch, for instance. He picked up a magazine, and it shouted at him through the din. The person who had written the words of the article he was "reading" seemed to be standing just behind or to the left of those words—he kept shooting glances here and there—shrieking and panting the longer the article went on. Each sentence seemed to take a year. Tears filled his eyes at the fruitlessness, the bootlessness of the writer's effort. To counteract all this frenzy and unnaturalness, he grew immobile and stared straight ahead. It seemed a reasonable thing to do, but this was what tipped us off. My eyes began to hurt as I watched him stare unblinking at the wall. He was either getting the details and missing the context or getting the context but missing the details. Everything was either sharp and meaningless or vague but full of impermeable content. Things slipped so suddenly for him, they veered so far and so fast, tumbling like a waterfall, that he cried out. He was in what he later called a state of raw prayer. He saw how sharp and meaningless his victories had been, how full of poison his soul was, and cried out, but was unheard in the roar of the party.

He faked lucidity for me as long as I stood talking in front of him but slipped away when I went to find Linda, who, when found and brought before Dennis, began sobbing almost immediately over his "refusal to make sense, because he seems very sensible, I must say!" That something unprecedentedly and unaccountably weird was happening to Dennis made the other partygoers uneasy. They became hostile and told me to take the fucked-up monkey away from them. I like to think that Dennis was living in the world they were only playing at living in, but of course I wasn't thinking that then, and wouldn't have said it anyway. Another guy from our squad—our big man who liked to get drunk and beat people up—and his girlfriend and Linda and I surrounded Dennis and eased him out the door, into a car, and back to his home, where we sat in a light blue living room, on plastic-covered furniture, holding on to each other for dear life. We were all white with panic, addled with druggy guilt, murmuring helplessly, hospital-quiet, heads hung low, unable to fill our lungs with air, waiting for a sound from his bedroom, a sign of recovery, a warning we were all prepared to hear, direction for a blameless life, a confession that it was all a bad joke, a request for water, anything. His brothers were with their mother, and his father was off somewhere hammering out an accord with the Episcopalians. We didn't know what to do.

He said he could hear the toaster working, the coils clicking, and then the toast being eaten. We'd all come down the hallway toward the bedroom where he lay listening to our unhappy breathing. Only I appeared in the doorway. Dennis began to tremble with some kind of electricity. As I drew near and sat down, that electricity overcame me as well. Dennis snaked an iron arm swiftly out from under the bright Mexican blanket and grabbed my hand. He said he had done terrible, terrible things. I laughed a stage laugh for everybody in the hallway, and asked him like what.

He stared at me for a long time. "I *will do* terrible, terrible things, then," he said.

I thought he was making a joke, and laughed again.

He told me to shut up and get out of the room before he killed me.

I laughed a third time.

"*What*," he demanded, "*you think I can't kill you?*"

"You don't want to kill me, Dennis, come on now. I'm your—"

"I could break your neck in a second!"

He began to think he was just dying, and that if in fact that was all it was, he was behaving very poorly, not dying well, as he'd imagined he would. He could hear what he thought was a large number of people out in the kitchen making and eating bologna sandwiches and instant coffee. The kettle screamed and screamed and screamed, and he confused death and birth, thinking we were boiling water for a birth. He grew determined to be helpful and die well, and listened carefully for hints.

We decided that if "things" with Dennis didn't improve in some quantifiable way, we would all go next door and throw ourselves at an adult. I had been fatherless for years, my mother was at our phoneless summer cabin, and Linda's parents, too, were on vacation, in Japan of all places! We didn't even know what Dennis's mother's maiden name was. And the other parents . . . we were sure these other persons would not understand somehow—even as understanding eluded us—being too close to us, but knowing Dennis only as a celebrity athlete whose father was a pastor and whose mother was a professor. The police were out of the question: they would bust everybody instead of helping us, and paramedics, it was reasoned, required blood, physical distress, in order for their sanction to be valid and their remedies to be effective. Our big man began to cry. Then Linda began to wail that "it" had happened only moments after she'd given Dennis a blow job.

Dennis felt he could see through walls now: the big man's head was in his hands and Linda had her hands held out imploringly as they shook in the rhythm of her weeping. *Blow job?* he thought. *You call that a blow job?*

I entered a second time and Dennis sat up, exposing a pale and stony torso, down which sweat ran like mercury. The ravines separating muscle from muscle were black and deep, black and deep, and he asked me again who I was.

"Dennis," I said, "I am your best friend, Lance."

He cried a good deal. Softly, while smiling. He said, "Okay, okay, I admit you look familiar, but I still can't say I know you."

I grabbed him and shouted, "WAKE UP! SNAP OUT OF IT! YOU KNOW WHO I AM!" I shook him so hard his head wagged on his shoulders, and when I stopped, his head continued to wag. He said he didn't know anybody within miles.

"Spare me," I said, as if I were on to him. "You know very well who we are."

The neighbor was not at home. We looked up and down the street at the other softly-lit suburban homes. We did not know if this was the sort of thing you brought to a stranger's door late at night or something you just rode out.

Just before dawn, he seemed to come around. He looked "tired but relaxed." I asked if he knew anybody, and he said he couldn't remember if he did or not. We all stood around his bed, talking lightheartedly. The big guy said that if Denny was feeling okay, he would split. Dennis said, sure, thanks for stopping by. I said I would stay the night, and that Linda might catch a ride with the other two. She knew she had to decide quickly and casually, but it took her a second to get going. We all watched her swallowing. Then she ventured the guess that she would go. Dennis smiled and nodded, as if pleased she was getting the hell away from him. We all went to the front door and Dennis crept silently behind us, hiding just around the corner. The big man and his girl walked out to his car. Linda came a little unglued and started groping me, kissing me passionately, thrusting her tongue down my throat. I wanted nothing like that from her, but felt ridiculously helpless to stop her.

Dennis and I were sitting on the edge of his bed. He needed to go to the bathroom, but things had deteriorated to the point where he was afraid to go alone. He really just wanted company, he said, and was extremely tired. He was wobbly on his pins after four years of victory and the hall seemed long and dark. We walked to the bathroom in a stately, ceremonial way. Once we were there, he flipped up the lid and let go thunderously, for a long time, as if he'd never pissed before, and as if nothing at all were wrong. But after a while I noticed that he was staring at me in the mirrors that went from floor to ceiling in that strange room. The halves of his face were rearranged. I looked away but he continued to stare at me. He didn't strike me as particularly angry or frightened, but he was staring rather intently. When he was done peeing and had snapped his Hawaiian-print boxers back up, he said the strangest thing. I don't know why he said it. He was kind of joking, again, kind of musing, kind of resigning himself, he said, to the idea that he was still dying, a provocative idea certainly, but it only made him feel weak and fucked up and ashamed and growing angrier by the second, and he said, "You're Death, aren't you?"

I said that I was not. I demurred politely, then a little anxiously, the halves of our faces rearranged for each other's mortification—because that's all it takes. I suppose he was thinking that of course Death would come in the guise of a friend who had lived a blameless, carefree life of taking interest and pleasure in every little thing that came along.

He walked over to me and began to strangle me. Then he threw me into the tub. I got out, awkward and off-balance, and he slammed me with a forearm to my head so hard that I saw stars. Then he dragged me into the hallway. I scrambled to my feet and knocked a picture of Dennis and his brothers off the wall. This got his attention and he stopped. He said he was sorry and rehung the picture, taking care to straighten it.

Demons departed and were replaced by doctors. He told them about the time he learned he would die. He was six, and it was in a dream. A hand came in through the window of a skyscraper, a big hand, and it came all the way down the hall. It kept on coming until it had grabbed his father by the waist and then it retracted, pulling him out the window whence it had come. He had seen a skyscraper only once or twice, as a thing that went up and up, a thing with an interior that in no way fit its exterior, a place his father and he had visited. But out the window went the pastor in a great suck of air that made the little boy's knees shudder. And he woke understanding he would die.

I didn't see Dennis for a long time. He wrote me two years later, and I will close with the last paragraph of that letter. *I did in fact have a vision of Jesus Christ, and it's everything it's been cracked up to be. The peace that passeth all understanding just keeps on going. I am sound again, even happy, single, spending all my time lifting weights (I broke the record for my weight by a full pound), crying out to the Savior, and taking drugs by the fistful. I want to live a long life, I pray, full of defeat.*

visigoth

I am a hockey player. That would be the first thing you
suspected about me. Though perhaps on second thought it
is not an entirely familiar pursuit. Hockey is a smooth violent sport played primarily in the cold blue silent reaches
of the North, where the report of a puck on wood at night
will carry for miles like fire from a high-powered rifle. I
am from Minnesota, which qualifies, and played to stand-
ing-room-only on the Keweenaw in Michigan, again an
easy qualifier. The players tend toward the bully and the
dumbbell; as for myself, yes, and yes again, Christ, yes, all
that and more. I had all my teeth until this time last year,
at which high-water mark they exploded from my gums
like tiny enameled angels, bursting in a rain of blood heav-
enward, released at last from this pit of woe, my mouth.

After the teeth, the Hobey Baker Award. What *is* the Hobey
Baker Award? The Hobes is a statuette given once a year

to an outstanding college hockey player. Unlike the Heisman Trophy in football, nobody gives a shit about the Hobey, and you only have to have one good year. In my case, freshman, which only made things worse, really. Of the ceremony I remember only that my remarks lasted an hour and that I shook hands four different ways.

I spent the summer thinking lordly thoughts. Rogue! Dark-browed prince! What next! I was ready for a martini with the business leadership as a slugfest with apes. Someone said the world was my oyster and I took it to heart. I'd committed apostasy, and I wanted it all. I did not want to be left behind.

Then I got hurt. My brain decelerated rapidly against my skull after my head got slapped to the boards at about a hundred miles an hour. My eyes rolled up in their sockets and I collapsed in a heap. Not a week later, I dove into the boards again and separated my shoulder. Skating gingerly in practice, sling in place, there was a miscue and somebody knocked me unconscious for a second time. My overlords treated it all in a light and manly way, judging it nothing to write home about but I knew better.

Ruth was my girlfriend. She came to me as an instructor of freshman composition. A poet at a technical university, she was amazed by my essay on summer vacation. She introduced me to William Blake but withheld Rimbaud, insisting that I learn the language. Ruth was an older, darker woman of twenty-seven, from New York City. What an accent! A real gypsy. If we discussed poetry, she would make reference to "Lowered Boyron"; if the weather, that it was "co-eld." She, of course, received no end of hoots over what I maintained was American Standard, saying I pronounced "Dave" as "Deve," and "napkin" as "nakkin." Anyway, we fell to each other easily and amused ourselves, for a time, simply by talking; louder, as that time went by, and louder.

Once, early on, just what you might expect, sophisticated city girl meets bumpkin musclehead, she tried to play dominatrix with me, but this backfired, bringing on not great desire but a terrible reflexive violence I caught and was able to turn back only in the nick of time. She said, I will not try that again, and I felt like someone not in control, not of his self or his destiny, someone in whom it was easy to bring out the worst.

Ruth bought my clothes for me. I had plenty of money, thanks to the Booster Club and the Chamber of Commerce Hockey Patrons' Discount Club, but I could not be trusted. I affected loudish punk cowboy attire, really a low-rent fashion zoo, and Ruth made me look good to a wide range of people, the widest range, really, people, honestly, from all walks of life.

I in turn washed her clothes, having a washer-dryer combo in the basement of the house I rented with one of my wingers, an Indian named Mikey Perch, the only guy from Wisconsin on the team, and the only Indian I know of playing hockey, though why I don't know. Mikey and Ruth liked each other a lot. Too much, I fear, but I have nothing in the way of evidence to back this fear up. Still, fear is fear. It is one of those things that brings out the worst in me.

I had a new Jeep as well. This was a kind of T-bone tied around my neck. Many in my collegiate circle lacked wheels, so I found myself racking up the miles not unlike nobody's business. Ruthie was a geology buff, and as you may know, the Upper Peninsula of Michigan is rife with ancient stone exposed for all to see, though many who pass know not what they see, and probably never do, the country being composed as it is largely of money-lusting half-wits on frenzied vacation. And even those who do see and know sometimes get lost in the figures. Confronted with gneiss at Norway Lake three billion years old, we revert to a childlike wonder that makes our eyes roll up in our heads and our teeth click in stifled yawns. Even to say that ten thousand years ago there was no Lake Superior doesn't really chill you the way you think it should. We go back a thousand, maybe two, before we lose the thread. I personally go back to the heyday of the barbarian nomads who invented the protosports that are now, in their mature forms, ruining us. The barbarians we are somehow given to understand we have "risen above." I don't get it. What is it we have that they didn't? Or what is it we don't have that they did? We live longer, have computers . . . and I know, I know, I know . . . if I were hurtled back in time and forced to be an actual Visigoth I wouldn't like it at all. Still, I look back and see their chief crime was that they were unnecessarily cruel to one another. Didn't speak Latin. Were greedy and limited in their arsenal.

Ruth had two looks. One was librarian and the other was Hebrew empress. If you are a subscriber to Time-

Life Books, maybe you have seen a picture of the former Josephine Marcus, wife for fifty years—you heard me, fifty—of mythic good guy/bad guy Wyatt Earp. She died in Hollywood, trying to sell the film rights, in 1944. The resemblance is there, you catch Ruth in the right mood and the right light. Josie left a bourgeois San Francisco home to pursue high life in the Wild West, and here again is resemblance. There was something about NYC that Ruth could not stand, and it is my belief that she never would have taken up with a hockey player—never mind *me*—had she not been somehow desperate.

Ten below and the snow is shooting horizontally past me, a hundred straight lines of it, tracks, effectively forming a wall, an infinite series of walls, that I fight my way through, making my way to Ruth's office, a nook in a temporary building that shakes when you open the door. My boots made big ominous noises down the plywood floor. I admired these sounds and thought as I banged down the hall, I will woo thee with my sword, Hippolyta. All the right myths were lit up in my head like Art Deco stations of the cross. A pinball game. Ruth and I were on the skids. Age difference.

She had her feet up on her old desk, the feet actually hidden behind tilting piles of blue books. Faint gray cathedral light fell from the high window on her powdery pink sweater, lighting up the kinky mass of her hair, neatly tied back with a pink ribbon. It was a peaceful, scholarly scene. She wore her glasses. But I did not care for it. In fact, it enraged me, a red flag. Last time I'd seen her, she called me an idiot, and I was brooding over the possibility. Meantime, I wanted to have her, there in the cool monkish cell, in the waning light. I wanted to slash the awful exam books and the horrifying poetry from the desk, heave her bottom up there as upon an altar, and make everyone in the building pause midsentence, look up from their books, and hear her Wagnerian screaming.

I closed the door and fell upon her, hands in her hair, tongue in her mouth.

She pulled away. Something like five seconds.

"I'm too busy, please, Neale."

Staggering, I said, "No, don't say that."

"I am."

"No no no. Please."

"Yes!"

"I want to have you. I must have you. Now. While the brothers chant. Here. On this desk."

"Find a cheerleader!"

"Cheerleader!" I gaped.

"I'm busy!"

"Cheerleader!" I said again. "Busy!"

"Go away!" She was half laughing but too angry for it to work. I mean sincerely angry, her eyes wide with disbelief. "Get out, Neale!"

"Ruth, I love you." I would have said something else but I think you get the picture: not altogether there, as far as good working order went. The only other thing I might have said was "cheerleader" again.

She sighed.

Sometimes, that's all it takes, a little sigh like that. You are as surprised as the next person. But there you are: at your worst. This is what plagues me today, what will plague me tonight, tomorrow, the rest of my life because I am an idiot, because I will not learn: How do you check the progress of an invader when he is in your camp before you know it? Sometimes the sigh in the shadows is all you will hear. What do you do?

I grabbed the nearest thing. It was a tall heavy book-case, an old oaken thing, finish gone, but intricate carving bracketing the shelves and along the front, fabulous crenels and merlons of a miniature battlement along the top, and Christ what a sinner, glass. I put my fingers between the back and the cold Sheetrock wall and pulled, stepping lightly away as it came.

It fell in perfect silence for a long time, like the last great pine, a lapse of hallucinatory seconds in which it was possible for me to see not my whole life in review but a good year or two of the arrogance and bullying that really set it apart, and then crashed against the desk, glass panes popping and flashing, a shelf splintering with a clear awful snap of cold dry wood, spilling volumes, the pages fluttering and whirring, dust rising, some heavier tomes smacking me in the face, now how could that be, the velocity is great, the pain remarkable . . . are they rico-cheting somehow . . . ?

No, it is Ruthie, pegging anthologies of American lit-erature at me. Underhanded, just heaving them up with all her strength. One catches me squarely on the chin and I fall down.

"Don't you ever fucking *sigh* at me," I said, infinitely pitiful, my wobbling, damaged head full of smoke.

"Animal," she said. "Criminal." It was true. She had her hands up now around her head as though fearing a blow.

"Sigher," I shot back. It was all I could think of. I was guilty and I knew it.

"Get out."

"I will get out pretty much when I want to and not a second before." I was just legging this one out.

"*Why did you do this?*"

Suddenly my brain let go and I had much to say. "I have no time for this quotidian *busywork*!" I shouted. "Round-table exchanges of reasonable views and compromise and balanced diets and designated drivers—you want sanity and routine, find a farmer! I'm crazy! I'm a star! I'm out of my mind! I'm tired of the virulent smugness of these people and their struggles to reconcile check registers with bank statements!"

"You *what?* You *what what what?*" She was up and at me.

"You heard me." I was overcome by loneliness and fatigue.

"You have lost it entirely!"

"I will not miss it for I do not need it." I wondered if I had any friends; and if not friends, enemies. Then I wondered what made one one and the other the other. I was so lonely I wanted to cry.

"It's irretrievable. You have ruined yourself and you don't even know it."

"Spleen, vigor, terror, and wonder," I said. "The Four Horsemen."

There was a knock at the door.

"Just a minute!" called Ruth pleasantly.

"I am ready to go now," I said.

"You were staring at yourself while you were kissing me, weren't you?"

There was a three-by-two black-and-white blowup of me on the back of her door, an action photo, very flattering, pretty much me at my best, defenders in chaos around me. "I wouldn't dignify that question—"

"Oh, just admit it why don't you? Don't be so goddamned pathetic! I can't take it! Four Horsemen!" She was shouting in spite of the student on the other side of the hollow door.

"—even if I could."

Whispering now, eyes slits: "Get out. Without another word if you can. You'll like yourself more if you just shut up and go away."

I went to the door. I put my hand on the knob. I couldn't look at myself. I thought, she's right, it's all over now. Crush the infamous thing!

I opened the door on a startled coed. Her fist was raised to knock. She saw the carnage and her eyes narrowed. Behind me, Ruth was picking up books and, ironically, whistling our song, "Body and Soul." I had three recordings of it: Coleman Hawkins, Benny Goodman, Lee Konitz.

"Hi, come on in," she said, her voice unnaturally high, accent largely missing.

I said to this girl, who remained standing there like she would not share a room with me, looking at me, God help her, me, whoever, like she knew me and what had happened, I said to her, "I go to pull Emily Dickinson off the top shelf and it exploded!"

Behind me, slapping books together, Ruth laughed, high and remote, the laugh, I don't say this to demean her, I'm past all that, but of a witch, the laugh of an innocent woman hung by ignorant savages in wigs.

I said, "I will go get that broom."

And Ruth said, "Oh, no, thanks, I've got one here, you just hurry and don't miss your class."

Three days later a just and merciful God spoke, saying, "The Destroyer of bookcases will be struck down and his mind and all the houses therein shall be made a dung heap. There will be blood everywhere. Hurt him."

One boy, a freak of nature from The Pas, Manitoba, five-six, two hundred pounds, something like that, swollen with muscle, face pure with the seriousness of his intent, this freak straightened me up against the boards and got the butt of his stick up under my cage and banged away at my jaw, the jaw already bruised and aching from the hurled books, rattling my imitation teeth. We were behind the play, no one was watching, and God, I sensed, had spoken to him, so he let me have it.

Then it got stuck up against my cheekbone. I jerked it out of his hands and skated away with it. Quick as I could, I flipped it to our team manager, Randy Curtins was his name, an engineering law major, and told him to cut the tape off the butt. Intuition, some sixth sense, I don't know, a little bird, told me there was pipe in there. In fact, I was bleeding but did not know it at the time.

People were yelling now, faces blackened with rage as usual, fans shrieking and chanting, players jostling, somebody had me pinned and was banging his cage against mine, spitting and shouting. "America!" I think, "Love it or leave it!" and the referee was demanding the stick be returned immediately. Randy was having a hard time with the tape and looked up hopelessly.

"You want to challenge, fine, I'll make the call and we'll measure the blade"—a blade can be curved only so much—"YOU STOP!" he bellowed at Randy. "RIGHT NOW AND GIMME THE BLANKETY-BLANK"—he actually said this, feeling strongly that obscenity on the ice was getting out of hand—"STICK!"

Randy handed it over.

I protested. But instead of seeing it my way and deporting the firepluglike zealot, he lost his temper and gave me two minutes in the box for unsportsmanlike conduct.

In the box, I got a towel good and bloody to throw at him when the period was over. Behind me drunken partisans jeered every which way. We were in Minneapolis, where I went to high school and where I first attracted the imagination of the steaming dimwits, and they hated me like the good homers they were. Then it became a little much and I turned to look at them.

They went wild. "He's looking at us! He's looking at us!" Many of them flipped me off while others shouted incoherently. One guy actually dropped his pants and mooned me.

I jumped up and cracked my stick on the glass, a big no-no.

The ref glided over and said over the cackling of the fans, "Neale, ding blast it, you ninny, that's ten minutes, go to the locker room." I skated off to thunderous hooting, escorted by a nervous lineman. "Dog doo-doo!" I shouted, to no particular avail or person.

My carrying the stick off was a grave insult that cried out for retribution and dirty violence of every description. After the second period started and my ten was up, I came out and it got positively shrill. Behemoths cruised the ice, aching for blood.

To make a long story short, I lost my helmet and a glove, then got jumped from behind and driven into the boards. All I could see was white for a second and there was nothing I could do. I blacked out and somebody . . . skated over my hand.

Mikey says I went in like I'd been blown from a cannon and was limp right away, bunched up in the corner, and Beausoleil (his name, Danny), borne on his own malevolence, followed me in, off-balance, and that was why my hand got skated on. It was not because he wanted to hurt me further. It was because he could not help but do so.

My hand, Christ, what a ruin. Christ alone would know. The first thing I saw coming out of it: floating in a lake of blood, a furrow cut across it, starting near the knuckle of my pinkie and angling slightly up toward the tip of the index. A groove, the flesh laid open like plowed sod. A little bone visible. Finger islands in the red lake.

And out again.

I am upstairs in the press box of an arena in a small city in southern Michigan. It is commanded entirely by trained

seals. The microphones before them each sound a different note. Right now, they are practicing "Row, Row, Row
Your Boat." Dressed casually, their glasses are opaque
with reflected light, their headsets suggesting, as far as
I am concerned, the insect world. From below issues the
steady roar of happy patrons; around me, the nasal barking and murmuring of critics and observers. My team is
taking on another, differently colored, team. We are the
Sled Dogs, they the Stoics. We use big sticks and a small
severed head. The score is 5-0, us, toward the close of
period one, a rout.

This is a terrible place. The main thing is that the game
can be seen . . . *without the obstruction of other people*, which
allows broadcasting. Coaches of minor grade perch here
because the great diagrams are revealed. These schemes
nauseate me; it is too easy for me to think of this as ar-
cade hockey on the big scale. From here it is only a tiny
prim hop to the horror of military miniatures and the
minds that are at work there.

There is a phrase we derive from English footballers:
a view of the field. The best players are often not the
strongest or the fastest, but the ones who have a view
of the field. Upstairs, with the media footmen and the
lieutenants, there is only the endless repetition of a few
basic patterns, and the slight deviations of random movements. When they stop to mill and posture, it looks like
any city street from a skyscraper office window: nobody
down there has any *power*, nobody down there has any
money. It is a false and pernicious view of the field. And
it rankles me, this sorry vision of my effort. Was I better
off not knowing?

I have not played for a long time. But my mouth still works, and everyone can feel the tension building; soon I will be interviewed. I want to do the right thing but my heart is silent in this matter. Not a peep.

I see Ruth everywhere but have not spoken to her, and I am thinking seriously of blowing off Writing of Poetry 101, having missed so many weeks now. It comes back to me all the time, what I did in her office, what I thought when I left it. That it happened so swiftly makes me dizzy. You can't apologize for a thing like that. If I were truly who I think I am, I would just go out and die with her name on my lips. Clearly, however, I'm not who I think I am. Next question!

I look around the press box. I am frightened by what I see: an angry race of seals who think I am Pavlov's dog. They're expecting drool, but they're going to get hot clouds of vomit.

The entertainment industry. Jesus.

To make matters worse, I walked to the arena the next day only to find the Ice Capades people setting up shop. I watched a leggy blonde cut some leisurely figure eights; after ten of them she glided to a halt, put her hands on her hips, and sighed audibly. I was a good fifty feet away and I saw her bosom heave and heard that sharp little bark of despair. Idly, I imagined myself giving it to her, the whole nine yards.

Three workmen, placing their tennis shoes flatly and carefully on the ice, walked past her, carrying a huge papier-mâché cave above their heads. They were forced

to go around her and she didn't give them the time of
day. In fact, one of them actually asked, sarcastically, I
think, *for* the time of day, and still didn't get it. I thought
reflexively that I was hot on the trail of an injustice. And
for the working class to boot! Then someone called her
name, "Phoebe!"

Onto the ice shot a slender young man in a tuxedo-
looking pair of tights. He raced around her, and then they
soared down to the far end, he singing a bit of a Sondheim
lyric. Down by the goal, which hadn't yet been removed,
he capered, legs flying, voice echoing, and I was overcome
by an urge to destroy him. To sweep in and hack at him
with my stick. I imagined the look of hurt and surprise on
his face as the first blow cracked across his shins. Later,
the sighing girl would cover him with her body and beg
for mercy, which, of course, I could not grant, not in a
million years, not honorably.

Blood smears the ice. I circle them, snarling. I am at
war with myself. I want his woman, and I want to kill him
for her, and yet . . . a great part of me does not want any
hard feelings. I simply want him away. But her too.

Why?

Do not want ice desecrated with sequins.

I was smiling through all this. I knew that. I was smiling at the woman. Sex is only the tip of the iceberg, but
what can that possibly mean? What I'm saying is that some
of this was just alpha male in the presence of a desirable
female, a silly interloper, and three breast-beating clowns.
But not all. I leaned over and laced my skates. I had no
plan but I would enter the scene.

My boy flung his arms majestically about and shook his fanny to the tune, neck tendons taut and his mouth an O. His circles grew smaller and smaller until at last he threw his skates out and slammed to a halt, the falsetto piercing me to the bone. Still singing, he glided a few steps and then set himself awhirl, the way they do.

The sound from his tiny siren of a mouth seemed to oscillate as he drew in upon himself and became a blur. I put my hands over my ears.

The workmen rolled their eyes and trudged gingerly off, jostling each other, trying to make each other fall in front of the female. Who stood center-ice, one skate cocked prettily, applauding, slapping her palms crisply together, fingers never touching. But who looked less than happy.

I climbed over the boards and ticked along the ice. I dropped a puck clacking to the ice and swooped down upon them.

The guy stopped singing when he saw me coming but didn't move. I blew past, sliding the puck past his skates and picking it up on the other side.

"Are we in your way?" he asked.

I passed through an arbor trellis with plastic flowers climbing it and came back to them.

"What?" I asked, coming in pretty close.

He looked at me for a long time, neither smiling nor frowning. Perhaps at some point he had won a bronze medal. The female lightly touched his elbow.

I longed for him to hit me. But the blow, I feared, would be weak, and that would infuriate me. At the same time, I longed to leave these innocent people alone.

"What's the deal, guy?" he asked, turning slightly away from me. "You some kind of hockey bully?"

That was it! I wanted him to tell me who I was!

The girl looked down in a minimal kind of move, eyes motionless, chin dropping a centimeter. I looked at her, and it appeared to startle her beyond all expectation, as if she knew something I did not. Perhaps, who I was!

"What *is* it?" she demanded. "Look, the ice is ours now. Can we help you with something?"

When I didn't say anything, the guy began to steer the woman away, saying, "Let's go, Phoebe, shall we?"

I slipped the blade of my stick over his shoulder. Hooked him. He slapped it off in a rage and spun around. I put it around his hip and yanked him to me. Nose to nose, I said, "You do this for a living?"

"FUCK YOU!" he shrieked. "FUCK YOU, SPORT!"

I dropped my stick and—even though I was the aggressor, had started it all, was guilty beyond reckoning—popped him in the solar plexus.

I sighed. It was my turn. "You asked who I am. We are animals here. Now we know. Show means nothing to us here. Glitter is extravagance and wasted. We respond to primary color and basic sound. We are pagan but fiercely devoted. When the stars look down and chance to spy us, they favor the animal. Time stands still for us when we engage our enemies. You ask who I am. I am an animal serving God and country *in a way that only I can*. I have the courage to be myself when I know I am loathsome. I am great and terrible and unwanted. But I am wondered at, am I not? Okay, who was I paraphrasing there in the last part?"

I left. They were speechless, of course. The guy couldn't get his breath back, and the woman—who could say what she was thinking?

For my part, I knew with certainty at last that I was beyond the pale. I would end in a madhouse, it was sure. I could see it all, the room, the food—as plain as the hand I stared at in front of my face, walking across campus in narrow corridors of snow twelve feet high, corridors in which our low northern sun would never shine.

the
bouncers

Two men, mesomorphs, sat on either side of a red door. On the other side of the door, also red, two city streets intersected. One followed the river while the other bent downtown. The numbers on the door were white and looked as if they'd been applied with a big house-painting brush. A sign, also hand-lettered but more neatly, said *500 CLUB . . . OUR MUSIC THIS WEEK* followed by the days of the week and the band of the day. One of the two men was named John Burl, "Milton" or "Uncle Milty" to everybody but me, and the other was me. I am called Lance, which is my given name (though what my parents, a quiet Minnesota farmer and his wife, could have been thinking when they came to that decision, I do not know). So we were Lance and Uncle Milty and we watched the door. John was married and had been involved in some kind of graduate studies at an Ivy

League school, but that deal had come apart and he was at loose ends. I had been installing carpets for a while, then phone systems. There had also been a stint as a server of subpoenas and a coder of documents. None of these deals had hung together for me, either. Which is why, in précis, we were where we were.

We had been lounging and vaguely expiating since his return from New York, frequenting terrible sports bars and a road next to one of the runways at the airport, and happened into the 500 one night where the manager surprised us by being someone we knew from the old days. Our satisfyingly nostalgic conversation was concluded by an offer of employment.

"I already have a large black person to handle the assholes, but I am tired tired tired of sitting by the door every night and checking IDs." This was quite a long time ago, and he asked us if five dollars an hour sounded fair. "Please say yes. The rough stuff is at a minimum these days. It's cyclical in this neighborhood. If you want to get into a knife fight, you have to go to Palmer's. We go for months here without any sort of incident. Our music, for one thing, is folkier than it used to be, and the place is turning into a college bar. I regret the ambience shift, but the nonviolence dividends are indisputable. Have you been out of the state for a while? The drinking age went down and then it went back up and we get a lot of youngsters in here. The rule is, you card everybody. You get a guy who's thirty-two and he can't believe he's being carded, you tell him to please shut up and just give you the card. I want this place to have a reputation. You know what I mean. A

no-nonsense sort of place. You can get lit but not necessarily have to watch your step every inch of the way. Good
music, fancy beer if you want. You know."

We signed on without even glancing at each other.

First night, a baptism of fire. An asshole came in and
ordered an outlandish series of mixed drinks and bizarre
liqueurs. He leered at the bartender, Gary, and let his incredibly dirty windbreaker hang open to reveal a holstered
weapon of indeterminate caliber. Gary said something de-
murring and the asshole leapt away from the bar, holding
his jacket wide open. *"I want the drinks I ordered and in the
order I ordered them! I just got laid off and I'll take everybody with
me if I don't get the drinks I ordered in the order I ordered them!"*

Our large black person ("Beaver") snuck up on him and
rolled him into a little squealing ball and I put in a call to
the police. Then nothing for a couple months.

It was Tuesday, midnight, one degree below zero. Vehicu-
lar traffic was sparse through our intersection, and pedes-
trian traffic nil. The band was called FYI. They performed
(according to their manager, whom we were shortly to
meet, a fellow who routinely but helplessly altered people's lives) a kind of feedback-augmented neo-Muzak on
trombones. They called their instruments "backbones" and
it was eerily beautiful music that should have had a bigger
crowd listening to it. FYI finished their last set, loosened
their ties, and lined up at the bar. Our friend the manager
of the club came upstairs and said we were off the clock
so we lined up too. We drank shots of ordinary alcohol in
silence and let a philosophical pensiveness build.

John said, "There are signs we don't get. Do you believe that to be true?"

"Surely," I said.

"In nature. It's speaking to us all the time, right? 'The earth he heard had made a noise but it was no sound he knew, no language spoken . . . more a harsh shadow than a sound . . . a single note of retreat.' That's Eastlake. Language and information everywhere. In the air, in the soil—the Universe itself is in some sense raw information. You know what I mean? And we don't get it. Ninety-nine percent of it: it flies right through us. Even if we *hear* something, even if we *sense vaguely* that we are *being spoken to . . .*" John was making little quote marks with his fingers every other phrase, up and down and up and down. ". . . even if we stop and wonder uneasily for a second, we're bound to think that what's happening is that we are *forgetting something we were supposed to do.* You know what I . . . ? We go blank and then fall into a daydream or start worrying aimlessly. I was walking along the edge of a gorge in Ithaca last summer. Very beautiful, very idyllic. A narrow strip of woods flanking a steep gorge, a stream, a little waterfall . . . it's early in the morning, I've read the paper, had my coffee, the water is flowing musically, the birds are chirping with it, and I am whistling a merry tune myself. Life is *good*. I'm on my way to *work*. I'm *working* and it's *steady* and there is *hope for the future*. I take a dogleg in the path, and there on this immense tree stump, right at the edge of the path, on the lip of the gorge, this immense stump with hundreds of rings . . . is a huge pile of shit."

I smiled and shook my head no.

"Human poop. A big pile of it. And it had just rained. So it was soggy. I saw it and a chill, an actual fucking *chill* went up my spine and I thought, *who* is sending this message to me and what does it *mean*?

"It was a sign of something," I said. "Surely."

"You tell me."

"I don't think I can."

"I got to the class where I was an assistant teacher, and there wasn't anybody there. I go to the professor's office and I ask what is up. She glares at me. I ask her where everybody is and what I am supposed to do in their absence and she just glares! Finally, and this is a quote, she says I can go soak my head in a bucket of water for all she cares. Of course I appealed this decision and they told me I was a good teacher but that I was irresponsible to the degree they felt we couldn't go on like we were. They said they were sorry and I said you can't imagine what you are doing to me, the extent of the damage you are causing, my self-esteem, my *checkbook*, the *furniture van* is due to arrive tomorrow and my *wife* just got here *today* and my rental deposit—sorry sorry sorry."

"That was how they let you go?"

"That was how they let me go."

"Did you get any licks in?"

"I called the professor a fascist cunt and that seemed like a great thing at the time."

"Well, sure, it's something, at least."

"Then I got real sick. Dry heaves. Actually pooped in my pants. Sobbed in a motel tub. I keep harking back, though, to the tree stump and the message."

"But what could you have done differently? How could you have avoided it? Any of it?"

"I might have been better prepared. It might have been less painful then."

I was sure there was more to the story, but I let it drop. John seemed terrifically saddened by the telling, and sadness was quite rare with him. I was sad all the time, hypersensitive, more and more afraid of strange people and places, tears welling uncontrollably at the slightest kindnesses. At the door, I had to adopt a hard, evil regard to protect myself, glaring balefully and speaking to no one, while John chatted and joked. He had what is called "a winning way with people," even though we both knew he was profoundly a loser. Gary came down the bar to us and we ordered further shots and talked about basketball until the lights came up and the last patrons departed into the cold night.

Friends of the band and people who worked there lingered for a few minutes while we closed up the place and dealt with the money. A guy I'd seen out of the corner of my eye a couple of times that night came up to us, blinking in the terrible light, and we recognized him as yet another high school acquaintance. His name was Wayne Boehm, and he was FYI's manager. Coked-up and intensely jolly, he was beside himself with joy at having met us: the world was so small and we were surely fated to meet for a great purpose.

It seemed to me that Wayne had hit a zenith in the eighth grade. He was the kind of tough guy who was able to court persons from all cliques, who could make

a hostile gesture in the hallway seem like a nod of acceptance. Once, he tripped me on the way to homeroom. He
and some intimates laughed. I'd just won an intramural
wrestling tournament and had some currency, some influence among the cliqueless, so I came back at him instead
of continuing to class. The bell rang and my heart beat
with fear. Wayne said, "I heard you kicked ass, man, way
to go," and stopped me cold. He grabbed my dangling arm
and shook my hand. I stammered something and looked
into his eyes. Was he saying something else to me underneath the announcement of power? I nodded uncertainly
at the ring of thugs and then broke into a trot. I'd just
gotten a new wristwatch (for winning the match) and in-
voluntarily checked the time. My name trailed after me:
Lance. Whether in derision or amusement or simple recognition I could not say.

And there he was in front of me again. Babbling away.
Eyes brightly empty. He had been a powerful person but
evidently had been able to make nothing of it.

"FYI," he said. "What could it stand for? Fuck You
Irving. That's their true name. I have other bands as well.
You know Assmar? From *Lord of the Flies*? The fat kid with
glasses who gets killed because he can't survive in the wil-
derness? I got Sunny and Chair, too. They play here all the
time now. *Funny*? *Fuck*, man. I got 'em lined up at Laff Riot
because the eighties will be remembered as the decade of
standup comedy, you heard it here first. Sunny and Chair
can weight their show every which way, comedy or old
folkie, touching ballads, social commentary. Everyone
says specialize, but I think the worst thing they could do

is make a choice. On the serious classical jazz side, I got the Saint Paul Saxophone Quartet."

The club manager came up on the other side of the bar.

Wayne said, "I keep telling this dickhead he should book the quartet, but jazz, I fear, offends his concept of this saloon."

"Honking and tweeting," said the manager. "The place would clear out like *that*." He snapped his fingers. "*And no more Sunny and Chair. Ever.*"

Wayne turned his back on our mutual friend with a big sigh. "You guys want to be free of this man and his small thinking? I got lots of projects going. Honest, clean stuff. I'll pay you twice what he's paying you. *Don't look at me like that!* Money is not a problem! *You need work?* I got work. *I am rolling in dough.* Money is the fucking *least*, man, of my fucking worries."

The work consisted of taking crowbars and sledgehammers to the creepy decayed interior of an old house he'd bought in a creepy and decayed part of town, and then installing light and breeziness and modern fixtures. Wayne was never there. He'd waltz in with sinister or dazed professionals of music and related fields, throw open the refrigerator, and hand beers around, talking fast. Then they would all pile out as they'd piled in. Occasionally, a clear-eyed conservative might be spotted, introduced always as "a true working musician, a serious dude." Even more rarely we would be introduced to financiers. Sometimes these men would be dressed traditionally and well, and sometimes not. John and I would look up from the basement, through the bare ceiling beams, at these men clapping across the loose plywood sheets that served as a floor, and Wayne would shout names, and beer would fall to us, the soft aluminum cans indenting in our palms. The men would look over the edge of the plywood and see our round chalky faces staring up at them. Often they would say nothing, saluting with their cans, and John and I would return to the concrete wall we were slugging down, return to the wallboard and mud and tape, the spackling gun, return to the copper tubing, the torch and solder and flux, the acetylene flame pure and blue in the musty dusty dark. Wayne paid us in cash every Friday afternoon at three.

We kept up the greeting at the 500 for a couple of reasons I now see as equally suspect. Number one was, we did not want to become carpenter monks. For John, it was simple: he needed to talk to people. Talking freed him from thought. I was trying to face down a comprehensive fear, a fear of "unsatisfactory social exchanges" (so it was explained to me). I felt limited in my resources, limited to the point where I could not deal with rudeness, or even frankness, to the point where I no longer believed I could ever explain myself to the other party, to the point where I no longer believed the other party had the slightest interest in explanations, to the point where I felt violence imminent, not as a last resort but as the only resort, to the point where I felt violence inhering in every isolated incident, from a request for cash back at the bank to a lane change. I thought, I have to keep coming back to the door. If I stay in the basement now, I'll never come up.

Reason number two was, we were getting caught up in the idea of steady work, of working all day and into the night, eating simple meals and sleeping the good sleep of laborers, getting up and working. We also began to save our money. We were getting caught up in the idea of that, too. There was less and less we wanted—but we wanted the money to pile up. We began to compete with each other to see who could go the longest without an expenditure. We stopped drinking. John began to speak of leaving his wife, the first sign we might have perceived as "bad," while I spoke of leaving town. These comprised our preoccupations: the abandonment of responsibility and a thing we referred to as "the coast of Labrador."

John lost a small bet to me (we gambled with each other freely, but only with each other, and did not view the money as "spent") when he purchased a sleeping bag good to forty below and a fold-up cot. He handed me the ten and said, "Buy me a drink, will you? I feel I should celebrate."

"Why?"

"She left me."

"Oh."

He pretended to raise a glass. "No more hissing through clenched teeth. No more horrible skull faces. No more weeping all night. No more planning."

Sometime later, after having spent a great deal of money on liquor, John said, "I read somewhere that the ultimate test of a man is what he'd do if he knew he could get away with it."

I made a farting sound.

"What would you do?"

"I don't know. What would you do?"

"I don't know."

"Lie?"

"I suppose," said John. "I mean, I certainly do *now* . . ."

"Cheat?"

"That would depend on whom I was cheating."

"Say me."

"*No.*" John wagged his head in drunken certitude.

"Rob a bank?"

"*Yes.*" Equal certitude.

"Kill somebody?"

"Again I must say that depends."

"Of course, of course."

"If I hated this person and they deserved to die? Yes."

"I agree with you. But I think it would be hard to stop. Wouldn't it? Once you got going?"

"Maybe you're right," yawned John.

Gary walked by with drinks on a tray for some friends of his (there were no waitresses at the 500, and usually only service at the bar), and we plucked them off the tray. We downed them and smiled like idiots, foundering in dreams of impunity. Gary looked on as only the sober can. We produced our savings passbooks and extrapolated figures until last call.

On April Fools' Day, I went over to Wayne's and found him and John having coffee in the bathroom we'd tiled the day before. Wayne looked eager and dazed, as if he hadn't slept in forty nights, and gave off a tremendous rotting smell.

"We're going to construct a sound studio *here*," he said, with odd emphasis, as if he meant the bathroom. "State of the art, et cetera. You know anything about burglar alarms, Lancey? Billion dollars worth of jazz and shit. Fuck it: *why not armed fucking guards?*"

He left suddenly and returned several hours later with two Doberman pups. It was "for starters. To initiate the posture of security. Uncle Milty, you should go to the library and read up on security. We can do this ourselves. I'm *so sick and tired* of relying on other assholes, aren't you? People will always let you down if they possibly can. Always, always, always. You guys I trust. Plus, I'm devoting all my time to this. Everything else is on hold. We got a bedroom finished and this is now my home. I'm bringing my lady in. I want to start a family. Here's the bad news: I can't pay you this week. Can you start this bastard on faith? Will you?"

"Hell yes," said John, holding his coffee cup to his cheek as if listening to it.

"Shit-yeah," I said in the Northern manner, making it a single word. "We're having the time of our lives."

Wayne mostly talked, and we never saw his lady. Though we heard her stomping about angrily or crying at regular (it seemed) intervals. Hysteria was in the air like perfume. Visitors thinned out. In the background was a constant faint bickering.

The weather finally turned. The lakes melted. Wayne was finding money, and we got paid off and on. Then one of his cars was stolen. It was an old car, beat up and unreliable, a junk-hauling car, but its theft enraged Wayne. He became frightening in his wrath, acting at times as if he suspected we'd taken it just to torment him, and that he might kill us. When he got the call that it had been found, up north in the town of Motley, he pounded the hammer and rang the bell of ecstasy. It had been cleaned out (tools mostly and a pair of ice skates) and run into a ditch, but was damaged only in ways you couldn't tell from the older damage, and the Highway Patrol had towed it to the county seat at Little Falls, where it was being stored.

Wayne leapt about his half-finished home, called his lady, almost sobbing with relief into the phone, then called up to Little Falls to arrange retrieval of his car.

He was informed that yes, they had his car, and yes, he could pick it up anytime during business hours, once he'd paid the hundred-dollar towing and storage fee.

John and I watched his emaciated face darken.

"Wait," he said. "Hang on a second. The car was stolen. I didn't steal it."

We watched him nearly strangle on his rage while the other party responded to his observations.

"*I didn't leave it in the fucking ditch! Find the shitsucker who left it in the fucking ditch! Try getting him to pay the fucking towing and storage fee!*"

When he'd calmed down the next day, he placed calls to his district representative and state senator, speaking moderately of his incredulity and disappointment that such a ridiculous practice was sanctioned in the great state of Minnesota. Then he called the sheriff in Little

Falls and let him have it. He was assured that his insurance company would pay for it, but this meant little to him, as he had no insurance.

Finally we all went up there and got it. Wayne needed only one of us to drive, but said he wanted friends handy if he started banging heads off walls.

It was good to get out of the city. Even though the ten thousand lakes are all nearly suburban in character and density of population, we all still like to see the buildings go away, and farmland and trees make up the scenery. We talked recklessly of get-rich-quick schemes that ran the gamut from wild investments to convenience-store hold-ups. Wayne inspired this kind of thinking when he wasn't paranoid and easily angered, when he was merely edgy and resourceful and doomed, when it was clear where the money came from and fine that it did, when he was an "outlaw," and John and I were "hard luck cowboys."

I bought a nice fishing rod and a good tent. John was informed by his estranged wife that she was pregnant. We were clearly in the last days of our association, and Wayne came to us meekly and without funds. He wanted to ask a favor that would make everything better.

"Person X owes Person Y tons and tons of money. Person X is fundamentally a nasty little shit but is moving up in the world and thinks that this renders all debts to Person Y void. I promise you no violence will be involved. You guys are the last guys in the world I would put in jeopardy. Do you believe that? Because it's true. I just want you to be there with me. Wait in the car and smoke cigarettes so they see the lighters flaring and the smoke coming out of the windows. After five minutes—I've got it timed perfectly—you come and knock on the door. You don't even have to come in. The knock is everything. The knock strikes fear in people—*and particularly in Person X.*" Wayne laughed like a hyena for too long. "You guys look grim. I don't need to tell you that, right? You knock, the fear sequence begins, and I am out of there in less than five more minutes. You guys look so fucking grim. Not shittin' you. You really do."

I didn't think John looked grim, and I didn't feel I looked particularly grim, either, but it was disconcertingly pleasing to hear that we did.

We sat in the junk-hauler, feet surrounded by beer bottles and fast-food packaging, cigarette butts and empty oil cans, some jugs of antifreeze, jumper cables, three well-used hockey sticks, and some greasy blankets. It was midnight and we were in the western suburbs of the city. The windows of the car were open, and smoke, as we'd planned, drifted from them. There was nothing to hear but our puffing and the faint drone of traffic on the belt line a half mile off. Brief spells of wind went right through the trees, two big cottonwoods, which we sometimes called "talking trees," and the leaves rubbed and sighed. I saw a rabbit in a circle of pale purple yard light and pointed it out to John, who nodded thoughtfully.

"I wonder if there was any hidden treasure in this car," he said after a while.

"You'd think so, wouldn't you?"

"This is just silly, Lance. We should just go."

"Sure," I said. "You want to?"

He nodded, but we didn't.

The house had been dark when we pulled in the driveway. Wayne had gone to the door and knocked in a certain way. Then, soundlessly, there was a second dark form at the door. We heard nothing, and then Wayne was inside. We waited for a longish time.

"How long did he say to wait?" asked John.

"Five minutes is what he *said*," I answered.

"How long has it been?"

"I don't know." I tried to read my watch and thought of the hallway in the junior high school.

"I think we should go knock."

No lights had come on, no sound had escaped the house. Nothing changed for several minutes. And then we were standing at the door, feeling absolutely as frightened as we could possibly be, our whispered voices choked with fear and laden with panic-dripping obscenity. I touched the doorknob and we listened. John nudged me and I turned to him. He made a comical impatient face. I must not have returned it properly, because it fell and his eyes were very wide. We stood there for another few moments, watching ourselves wait and tremble and then the fear became anger and I was pounding on the door. We moved to either side of the door and watched it. The echoes of my pounding faded in the air, our ears, our brains. John sighed and tried the door. It opened.

We continued to stand there at the door, looking in but with our feet glued to the little concrete porch. After some time we called out. We called out discreetly but forcefully and tried to keep from squealing. We walked in—almost as if it were no big deal, we were just dropping by.

We found them in the living room. Wayne and Asshole X sat in opposite stuffed chairs. The conversation of death was still in the air. I half-expected to hear a tape recorder rewinding, the conversation replayed. John was hyperventilating and I squeezed a tiny amount of syrupy shit into my underwear. There was a large pistol on the floor near Wayne's limp arm. His mouth was pursed as if he'd been about to make a judicious point, and might yet. His eyes were half open, and he was staring at his lady. It took us a moment to recognize her because we'd seen so little of her, and she was now horribly disfigured, but it was her. She had a slightly smaller pistol in her hand. There was some blood, two dead lovers, a couple of hot revolvers, and a thick cylinder of rolled bills. John made a small choked sound and grabbed the money. "Wait," I said, "there may be more." And there was.

I never saw John again. I bought another nice rod and an electric trolling motor. We never got caught, but of course there are worse things than being caught. There is always the feeling that you have done something you should not have done, and that further, it had happened without warning. You were deaf, dumb, and blind, and did not know even the most trivial thing about yourself. You knew nothing, had no control, no control of any of it at all.

the
volunteer

"Few men realize that their life, the very essence of their character, their capabilities and their audacities, are only the expression of their belief in the safety of their surroundings."
—JOSEPH CONRAD, "AN OUTPOST OF PROGRESS"

William Axelsen, a young man of mild features and demeanor, possessed of no certain skill but well employed, given to musing inventories of himself and even to melancholy dreams of a skill and the violent or at least consequential and illustrious exercise of it, picked up another piece of firewood, oak split and dried so long it seemed weightless, almost feathery, and knelt with it before the stove. It was already extraordinarily warm in the little room—his wife had said so, absentmindedly or drowsily he couldn't tell, watching him bundle another load in from the shed they'd carpentered together, soundly and strictly for the purpose of curing wood—but comfort, as a measure of heat, didn't seem to be the point. He slipped on an oven mitt and swung open the stove's heavy little doors.

The roaring inferno of the full stove quickly moderated into a kind of muffled howl as smoke funneled up the flue and the wood crackled cleanly, giving itself up to light and heat. Bill watched the miraculous destruction with growing calm; the flames licking out at him were gentle, hypnotic. He said so, but his wife offered no reply.

He had been advised at work to pay attention to what his adviser called "the civic duty aspect" of his résumé. He agreed it was something worthy of his sincere attention but was troubled by the phrasing. Martha, his wife, worked for the same company. There were few who did not in their large upper-midwestern town. It was a good life of sophistication and safety in a cold climate that promoted tidy industriousness and Christian homogeneity—threatened only recently by the arrival of Hmong and Vietnamese and Puerto Ricans who immediately subdivided into murderous gangs and forced people to buy drugs. Bill and Martha believed themselves luckily employed, but that hadn't prevented Martha from characterizing the company as a paternalistic, hierarchical horror of technocracy where of course civic duty would be considered an aspect of a personnel file.

"Bill," she murmured as he forked and prodded the luminous crumbling splits around in the stove and stuffed another in. Then something he couldn't make out. The tone of it was vaguely unpleasant, the rhythm familiar. He wasn't sure and, strangely, did not want to know.

"I know, I know," he said, staring intently at the fire though his eyes were quite hot now. "If I were half the man I think I am, I would find another way."

"You are twice the man you think you are." Martha's saying so was not necessarily a compliment. "Close the doors now. My skin is blackening."

This particular conversation was, not surprisingly, a chestnut. In the end, they simply went to work and paid their bills—no matter how amazing, month after month, they might be. The thinking—if it could be called thinking—went like this: If either of them so much as blinked over the grindstone, they would free-fall to financial ruin. Disappointment with the way things were was as dangerous, to them, as the pipe bomb of a terrorist. If it didn't make Bill's and Martha's organs shrink with fear, it nevertheless controlled them utterly.

Almost, he sometimes thought, in direct but covert defiance of that control, he saved small amounts of money: rolled pennies, slipped plinking into a ceramic whale he'd fashioned and fired himself, pocketed ones and fives like a waiter his tips—thinking that this was somehow money that nobody knew anything about. He had in effect happened upon this money. Nobody had a claim on it, or a lien. Occasionally with this money he bought flowers, or, if many months had gone by in strict adherence to the budget, earrings or a blouse or a pair of shoes. Whenever he presented such gifts, it was with an air, more comic than not, of having stolen them. Once, he seemed as nervous, actually pale and sweating, as if he'd stripped a dead woman.

He closed the doors of the stove and flipped the locking handle back in place. The little bimetallic coil thermometer stuck with a magnet to the top of the stove showed an arrow rise through green, yellow, and orange zones, pegged in the red. I either, thought Bill, need more of it or less of it, because this is not right. He looked at Martha as if in sudden and authoritative answer to a question nearly lost to memory, but she had closed her eyes and tipped over on the couch, apparently so overcome with drowsiness or fatigue or depression she'd not bothered or been able to remove the newspapers from beneath her. I am either in control of my life, concluded Bill, or not in control of my life. I can't tell the difference.

Bill had volunteered as a coach of the very smallest of the organized hockey players: Mites, they were called, and Squirts, fierce and driven five-to-eight-year-olds. It was already, he knew, a business like any other, "a game" only if he must, but really only metaphorically, high stakes in any case, deeply and oddly and perhaps shamefully American. Many of the little boys already understood that it was now or never, in some way they could not articulate, and Bill told himself that he liked them—liked them generally, of course, but liked them especially for *it*, for the self-knowledge, the uncomprehending focus—that was how he put it to his co-workers—the energy and the ambition so consuming it seemed, in children so small, so young, otherworldly. These were qualities the confused young manager of information believed he lacked, and so he tried to admire them humbly and hopefully. But when he caught himself thinking freely he found he resented them, the children and their parents and their dubious superiority. This resentment threatened a precarious and indignant sense of altruism, as well as a warmheartedness he had been encouraged to think was central to his personality, so he dismissed it. Consequently he felt nervous, and knew this nervousness would be like a little beanie with a propeller atop his head, as far as the children went. Still, he'd volunteered.

Gently he pulled the newspapers from beneath his nearly snoring wife and paged through a catalog of fall fashions over which she'd exclaimed uncertainly.

An early blizzard, of national note, failed to shut the town down, and did not prevent most people from attending a Halloween party. The partygoers were mainly professional people: a few doctors, grumbling under the boot of the big insurers, some lawyers filing antiquack and product liability suits right and left, trying to stiff the big insurers, and a handful of nutty professors from the private college on the edge of town—but the vast majority were managers for the company, managing they often knew not what, but managing anyway, in the best sense of the word, "hanging in there," they told each other tirelessly, waiting all the while rather anxiously for final word on a possible relocation for the superconductor facility, and effectively for the whole company, lock, stock, and barrel. Kentucky and Tennessee had been mentioned as top candidates, the speaker's lips curling in an odd rendition of a generalized "southern accent," cut heavily with xenophobic sarcasm and a bitterness born of fear.

"Do you even *like* hockey?"

The party had lengthened, accelerated, and been transformed. Before Bill stood an attractive woman in a tight red dress. He had never been introduced to her, but realized that she had been in the back of his mind for many months, if not longer. The music was loud enough to allow or require an intimate stance, and he adopted one naturally and easily. Her surging hair brushed his face when her gaze was swept momentarily elsewhere. Her perfume remained about him. She was, he knew, after a few seconds, the wife of the man who would be coaching a team of Pee-Wees and a team of Bantams, slightly older boys who were already using weights and being scouted by high schools in the bigger, wealthier suburbs of Saint Paul and Minneapolis, where well-funded programs turned out a surprising number of professional players.

"Do I even like hockey was I think the question?"

"I do not," said the woman. Her name was Debra. Debra was very sexy, Bill thought. She held his shoulder while she spoke, leaning in closer and closer. Her husband, Garth, had played college hockey and was very good, very big, and very fast.

"I love hockey," said Bill. He spoke with the simple dignity of a man who would not be seduced. "I really and truly love the game." He was going from lips—where he watched the muscles around her mouth move—to flashing earrings dangling back and forth at him like semaphores in the middle of the night as she moved her head nearer and farther against the hazy swarm of color behind her. Then it was décolletage and hips and long legs and high heels and back around again. She was sharp but friendly, open in a way that didn't quite parse with sharpness, and that was effectively spellbinding. Within the confines of this spell, Bill told Debra of his career as a player in high school in the southern part of the state. It was a wrestling town, he said, of all things, below the hockey line and the program was therefore a joke, but Bill had enjoyed a reputation as a swift and agile athlete, and, more importantly, as tough, in the crazy way, it was readily understood even there in the midst of the wrestling farmers, that only hockey players could be. He was not quite as big as Garth, certainly, and if he wasn't exactly fast anymore—if he never really had been *fast*—he was good on his skates and slick with the puck.

"It's a redneck sport," said Debra without seeming to give offense. "Rock'em Sock'em robots."

"Garth seems to think highly enough of it."

She ignored this. "Give me basketball any day of the week. There are your superior athletes. Oh my yes! The *squeak squeak squeak* gets on my nerves and I don't enjoy the triumphant hostility that comes of *making a basket*— they do it so often! But still . . ."

Bill dreamed vaguely of a hard-drinking cocktail party lifestyle he'd never actually been privy to. He was not at all sure where he'd picked up the notion, certainly not from his parents or Martha's parents—probably from a short story by John Cheever or John Updike, but he couldn't positively remember reading these short stories. Those were the names, though, that came up as he imagined a riot of repressed conversation and sudden chemical imbalance that would propel him into a bathroom or a closet with the woman before him. He'd never cheated on Martha and was sure he never would—but he wanted to, he was clear about that, and in the riptide of real cocktail party from another time in another place, it would happen of its own accord.

"Lots of basketball to be had down Tennessee way," he said. He was still thinking *riptide* and *commuter trains*.

"Oh!" said Debra loudly. "Oh! Now he throws Tennessee in my face like I'm some kind of traitor! *Traitor!*" she cried. "*Listen.*" Closing down alarmingly, she hissed, "We have no children and I am sick to death of this place. Do you understand? I would go to *Tennessee* in a—in a *New York second.*" She snapped her fingers quite near Bill's nose, so that he crossed his eyes and pulled his head back. But as if it were part of a charm she was working on herself as well as Bill, she opened up beautifully again. "Do you have children?"

"No. I too would go to Tennessee in a second."

She laughed pleasantly and volunteered to drive. When Martha appeared at Bill's side, Debra declared them twins, cute as could be, one dark, one light. They had in fact come as the Sun and the Moon, the big yellow and little silver masks held now by Martha before her like shields. "But looks," said Debra, suddenly (apparently) drunk, "wow, they're so deceiving. I have never been more beautiful, have I?" she asked with a sneer that could easily have seemed rude to Bill, had it not been so disturbingly exciting, and walked away.

The next day they sorted bills and found they were a little short. Bill brought in a load of firewood but as he stamped snow from his boots Martha asked that no fire be built. She wanted the room cool, wanted to wear a sweater. Bill went out, not angry but disappointed in a peevish way. Thinking he might return to the sport of hunting after years of neglect following the death of his father—acknowledging seriously and with surprisingly little ambivalence an idea he remembered hearing as a very small boy, that "killing can take a lot of bullshit out of a man"—he walked the several miles from his new "suburban" home to the hardware store downtown, where he priced deer rifles and multi-choke shotguns. He had two fifties in his pocket, crumpled and wadded like old ones, and did not, he was sure, seem like a real customer to the sales clerk. Returning home, the sun set and the temperature dropped swiftly. And while he knew he was in no real danger—the road being well traveled even on a cold winter's night—the idea that he might slip on some ice, break a leg or an ankle, be overlooked by passing motorists, and die of exposure in his light fall jacket was one he found he could not, as he walked swiftly but carefully, easily shake. His own great-grandfather had nearly died walking from barn to house, had he not, in those early years in the new land . . . ?

Bill and Debra met accidentally two or three days later at the town's coffee shop. It had remained very cold, but the sun was shining and the sky was a brilliant and pacific blue; nestled in the mounds of glittering new snow, the café seemed a nexus—if not the essence, the apotheosis—of all the comfort and warmth and reassuring security a prosperous and tidy town could afford its citizens. Consequently, Bill felt lively. He and Debra chatted laughingly for an hour, then agreed to do it again sometime soon, which meeting occurred at the end of that week, after Bill wandered rather far afield on the company's sprawling campus and less accidentally ran into Debra, in her office. At the café they spoke of matters that became with each passing minute more and more intimate, venting the building pressure with heartfelt chuckles and the admission that it was "great to be able to talk to someone like this."

Walking to the doors, Bill saw himself unflatteringly reflected in the glass. It was an undistorted image—not a funhouse mirror—but the features the glass chose for prominence and definition, these were not the features Bill would have chosen. In fact they did not seem to bear any resemblance to the image he had of himself.

When he pushed the door open, twisting more awkwardly than he would have liked to allow Debra passage, a tremendous blast of cold air entered the café. Debra exclaimed and the pages of a newspaper on a nearby table fluttered. Several people looked up, faintly alarmed looks on their faces. Bill blinked, then apologized, pulling the door closed behind him.

The manager of the skating facility (a park board employee who had a degree in it) handed Bill a thick gator-clipped stack of application forms, all filled out, some in adult hands, several in grade-school giant-size letters tilting comically, animatedly here and there about the form, each with a check stapled to it. "My boys there on top," said the manager (rather sternly, Bill thought). "Axel five and Troy eight." Bill remarked that his father's name had been Axel and his father before him, too. "I'm William the first," he said, grinning. The manager stared at him. Axel and Troy, Bill noted, were both "defensemen." He wondered, in the wake of the manager's humorlessness, if that meant they were both fat or that neither could skate. The manager turned and handed another stack of forms to Garth, who had just entered, skates already on and therefore towering above them. As they walked down the rubber-carpeted steps to the main floor of the arena and the rink, Garth said, "I wish I knew what you said to Deb at that party! She's just been loopy about college basketball ever since. It's all over the cable channels and she won't do anything else!"

Garth laughed but Bill did not. Garth's reputation as a wit had always struck Bill as undeserved, the wit sophomoric at best—locker room wit. "We must cross the Great Ohio Desert to get to the Promised Land of Kentucky!" he'd intoned at the party, and Bill had found it impossible to pretend he was amused. He'd never been to Ohio but he was sure it was no more poor in culture or in natural beauty than the other forty-nine.

Bands of tiny skaters roamed the ice. They all wore bright jerseys advertising various products, many of which had nothing to do with hockey or even sport.

The smallest appeared to be all helmet and skates, like cartoon characters who'd just had sixteen-ton weights dropped on their heads. Parents, older siblings, relatives, and a reporter from the local weekly slipped cautiously around the children, conversing in the harshly bright light with folded arms. Several games of tag were in process; the little boys were down more than they were up, but when they were up, Bill saw, they were moving at a pretty good clip. Sometimes a tag would be made with a stick, followed by a wail of protest and a show of psychotic Cupid faces, the scene concluded with amused rebukes from Mom or Dad. One stout overseer went to his hands and knees en route to a pileup and was applauded by everybody in the place while he picked up the pens and pencils that had spilled from his pocket. Even the children stopped fighting. It seemed unduly momentous. The man stood and bowed in four directions. While Bill and Garth checked their stock of equipment and went over the morning's schedule with the manager, one of the adults spread his legs wide, instantly funneling Mites, Squirts, and even some of the smaller, goofier Pee-Wees through this squat breach of corduroy. They would bear down as fast as they could and at the last second throw themselves to the ice, sliding through the man's legs on their stomachs, piling into each other—blades flashing— against the boards on the other side.

Bill looked at them, unmoved by the good cheer. They were fundamentalists, willful and intolerant. It was "a hockey town" and the parents, in the absence of a dominating tyrant, ruled.

"Don't be afraid," said Garth, as if reading his thoughts, "to ask me for help."

After the manager found his mike—it *was* a show, he *was* the MC—he asked, now rather obsequiously, Bill thought, for quiet, and introduced the two coaches: Garth Miller was justly well known to many of them, and Bill Axelsen had played in the Minnesota state tournament on the surprising Albert Lea team some years earlier.

Bill was startled: he had never played in the state tournament. It was a pure, bold lie, a powerful one, and he could feel its effect rippling like magnetism through the people around him. A player from the far north who'd been on the Soviet-smashing Olympic team, an NCAA championship team, and a Stanley Cup–winning pro team, had once told a reporter from *Sports Illustrated* that there was nothing like the state high school tournament. It had been the pinnacle of a long and happy career.

Many people felt that way. As parents filed off the ice, one of them wanted to know what year that had been when Albert Lea had been so surprising, but Bill pretended to have misheard the question as a compliment and skated off with his whistle blasting. The parent was the engineer who'd slipped, and he stood there watching Bill skate away, still faintly red in the face, eager to take issue with someone and not fall down.

They finished that day of basic drills with a chance to practice "breakaway moves," the little snipers coming in alone on Coach Bill, who handicapped himself by closing his eyes. When it was all over, a sweaty bright hustler named

Brad, who seemed to have sensed the tentativeness of Bill's situation in a sympathetic way, skated up to him, slammed on the brakes like a big boy, and said, "Good game, Bill," tapping him on the shin pads with his little stick.

Garth swung by. "Fuckin' beats basketball any day."

"Basketball," agreed Bill, "is for tall people."

The manager, now on skates too, joined them, hoping for "a little two-on-one?"

Garth and the manager looked at Bill with a kind of sincerity that prevented him from checking the time. "Sounds good!" he said instead, though he suddenly understood that his interest in hockey was waning. They played on the powdery creased ice for ten or fifteen minutes. Then someone shouted from the glassed office high above the rink at the far end that the manager was needed on the phone.

Bill looked up over his shoulder at the head behind the sliding glass window, a bald head, the window closing between him and it, the shout still in the air, the manager wheeling abruptly and hopping from the ice through the big Zamboni gate—he heard the puck click against the boards behind him. It was a moment of tremendous ennui. Then Garth Miller hit him at something like thirty miles an hour and flattened him; if he later concluded that he had not actually lost consciousness, he did see stars and lose, for a moment, track of things.

Bill collected himself and then considered the hot, deep pain in his rib cage. He was convinced that a prank had been played and looked dizzily around the rink for evidence confirming this suspicion. But there was none. He was alone. He rolled to his hands and knees and made bright red spots on the soft white ice. The bald man at the far window popped up again and opened it. He leaned out and hollered his concern. Bill waved that he was okay and got his skates. Then once again out of nowhere Garth appeared, helping him up and murmuring strangely something like an apology. It was almost as if, Bill thought later, Garth was helping him up and warning him not to get up at the same time, with the same words, in the same dull tone of voice. When Bill insisted he was fine, Garth skated off.

Bill found him sitting on a metal folding chair in his underwear, staring blankly at his bag of gear. The lights of the locker room had not been turned on; a thick gray light could be seen in a row of high small windows beyond the last row of lockers. Bill sat with dramatic care on a bench opposite Garth.

"I'd like to go over that last little deal there," he said after a while.

"Which?" Garth asked absently.

"That last one."

"Drawing a blank."

"The one where you drew blood?"

Garth finally looked at Bill. "Oh man, hey, sorry. Didn't see you in time. Heard Baldy shout and ouch, your nose." Only Garth's mouth moved, and Bill found himself watching it. Then he suggested, in that strange atmosphere of deprived or selective sense, that it had been a cheap shot, designed and executed solely as such.

There was no demonstrable change in Garth's demeanor. "No such thing," he said, "as a cheap shot where I come from."

"Yeah?" Bill actually laughed. "Where do you come from?"

Garth laughed emptily.

"You blindsided me."

"Blindsided?"

"I didn't see you coming and you—"

"You didn't see me coming and that's *my* fault." He snorted. "Wake up. You want me to get the smelling salts?"

Bill thought, What is this all about? Should I have not spoken to his wife? Did she say something provocatively nice about me? I don't take hockey seriously enough for this has-been, what? Should I have not had coffee with her? "What?" he asked out loud. "I'm seeing stars and spitting blood and you're skating off with your hair still nicely groomed. Your pal the manager hears the boards crack and the glass rattle but he's got to take that call? Talk to me, Garth, I don't get it."

At the mention of his name, Garth seemed to come around to sympathetic recognition of what had happened. He shook his head vigorously, as if clearing it. He smiled ruefully. "Christ, I'm sorry, Bill buddy. I don't know why I unloaded like that. I really don't. It's not you, it wasn't personal. Hey, I saw the shot and I took it. I get on the ice and the old ways, you know, they don't die, I guess . . ."

Garth stood up suddenly and Bill flinched visibly. He wasn't sure if Garth had noticed the flinch but felt he must have: it was the kind of head jerk one associated with falling asleep in an airport—or rather, being rudely jolted from a reverie, a half dream, from lulling alpha waves on the edge of sleep to a pounding heart and an unidentifiable noise in the darkness.

Garth rummaged in his bag—that was all he'd intended, it seemed, to find his bag. "Here, bud, have a cigar. Peace offering?"

He reached the cigar across to Bill, who could see it was a decent one that wouldn't blow up in his face. He took it and said, "I hope the old ways don't come back when you're skating with the kids."

Garth unwrapped his cigar. "You are absolutely right to say that to me." He found some matches, then his billfold. From the billfold he produced a fifty-dollar bill. He showed the bill to Bill as if he were about to perform a magic trick. Then he lit the cigar and held it to the fifty, puffing hard. The bill caught and began to burn.

Bill felt, dizzily and unhappily, that his back was against the wall. He couldn't figure the proper response quickly enough: contempt for a knucklehead by ignoring him and taking a shower? Or should he accept the challenge and go him one better? Was his message to be that burning money was the foolish gesture of an insecure man? Was it in fact foolish? Or was it merely empty, a meaningless act to someone who had his priorities straight? What are my priorities? Bill couldn't think quickly, decisively enough. He felt foolish, unmanly. He went to his locker and found the balled-up fifties. He straightened them out as if they were symbols of priority and showed them to Garth. "Not photocopied," he said. Then he leaned carefully over for the matches, groaning a little for effect, struck one, lit the limp bills, and watched them burn.

After the silent shower and the silent dressing, in the careful musing silence of imminent departure, Bill stared at the ashen currency on the rubber floor. What had he done? It seemed so reckless and stupid, inexplicable and—he stopped dead—unforgivable. He drove home, slowly but dangerously, almost blindly, watching chaotic thoughts and indiscernible images loop endlessly past what he could not help but think of as a grotesque and horrible inner eye, an amoral but ravenous and unblinking incubus. What had he said to Debra that was so refreshing and illuminating? What had she said to him that made him feel so invulnerable and wise? It was as if the man in the reflection in the glass doors of the café had been speaking and listening and commanding his body while the Bill he thought he was slept and dreamt troubling dreams. I am a volunteer, he thought as he pulled into his garage and entered his house, and that is a good thing. A man who has his priorities straight can always find the time to volunteer, because he knows he will always get back much more than he gives. It's a wise and solid investment in something that matters. The dividends of real joy are often overwhelming.

Martha crouched before the stove. Her face was smudged with soot, through which tears had clearly run. She laughed sadly, thinly, and said she couldn't so much as light a fire and therefore had no business being alive on the planet.

Although Bill did indeed feel overwhelmed, it was not
with joy. He understood himself to be a different kind
of volunteer altogether. It went back to a time when the
ranks were filled with the criminal, the abandoned, the
brokenhearted, the mad, the desperate.

He was, in some way he could not articulate, free. He
tried to think about this strange overwhelming sense of
freedom in a way that evaded the glare of the monstrous
inner eye, but the room was cold. He could see his breath
and he could not stop shaking.

the flight
from california

1

Three of us started out on a journey. Two of us came back. We began with a kind of amusement park ride. I used my Ford Escort wagon—a '91, bought used in Needham, Massachusetts, in '98 for the sole purpose of removing my wife, Leslie, and myself from our home in Mansfield, Connecticut, to our new home in Redlands, California— to go up and down and around and around the San Bernardino mountains. My plan was to get to the other side of them, descend into the Mojave, and flee California. My dream was to never return.

I loathed California. The only consideration that tempered my loathing was strong, vivid memories of loathing Connecticut when I lived there. I said things like, "Had I only known . . ." but the truth was, well, I don't know what the truth was. My guess is that I had a fixed idea regarding places where I could live and not be filled with loathing. It was also not lost on me that California was a big state. When friends (in loathed Connecticut! as well as beloved Minnesota) asked me how I was liking California, I would say, "I love San Francisco. San Francisco's great. It's really expensive to live there, though. L.A. is like a negative of the setting sun, a black and spreading ellipse on the horizon." (I really do talk like that, at least I do when I take my Prozac or whatever the hell it is I'm taking now—the letters and numbers stamped on each pill, I can tell you, suggest a smiley face.) "The Inland Empire," I would continue, "where I live, is a special part of the Southern California experience: Riverside, San Bernardino, Ontario. Its main claim to fame is that it's the road rage capital of the world. And even if we aren't exactly enraged, our highways are dangerous places to be. There was a two-hundred-car smashup the other day. It started raining, you see, and everybody got disoriented. The most interesting aspect of the incident was that it was actually a hundred separate accidents, rather than one big one. It was as if drivers were pairing off. Like in some support group or seminar where you have to turn to the person next to you and introduce yourself. But instead of shaking hands and grinning, you lock bumpers at eighty miles an hour. Ambulances arriving for the first round of wounded became embroiled in the chain reaction. We were lucky insofar as no one died. Very often on that highway motorcycle cops will shoot past, signaling disaster ahead. Traffic will slow and then stop. Helicopters appear on the horizon. Quickly overhead, they begin to drop like vultures to feed on corpses."

Mountain roads of course are nothing like "the Ten" (all highways must be preceded by the definite article, and often go by names rather than numbers, à la the Harbor or the Golden State or the Santa Monica); rather they are terrifying in their own way. The density and turbulence of flow on them can sometimes be indescribable, as skiers, hikers, and daytrippers seek relief from the smog and heat of the valleys—and all it takes is one low-powered economy car, or heavily burdened van, or motor home (why are these things so often nicknamed "The Stalker" and "The Prowler"?) or tractor-trailer rig, or slightly less than hell-bent driver, to slow traffic to a crawl. The notion that mountains must be climbed at a crawl—because they are big and steep and we are small and weak—assuages no one. We are no longer weak. We have high-speed tanks to get us to the lodge.

If you choose to drive during periods of time when statistics indicate drops in volume, then you are prey to the large trucks of mountain men who are taking advantage of the open roads as well. These fellows can be identified outside their vehicles by their caps: they wear them bill-forward. This is a symbol of the seriousness with which they engage their marble-hewn lives. They may get their firewood from kindling.com and their news from CNN but by god they are not illegal aliens, they work for a living, and a bill keeps the sun out of your eyes. The traditionalists among them wear their beards very long and will threaten to piss on you if you ask them to turn off their security lights at night, or for at least part of it. They can go from Redlands, most of which lies about thirteen hundred feet above sea level, to Forest Falls (the canyon village in which we were living at the time of this story), at six thousand, at a hundred miles an hour easy. The grade varies, but basically you're climbing forty-five hundred feet in about fifteen minutes even in a Ford Escort. Mountain men cut that travel time in half. And woe betide the operator of the little Ford wagon who doesn't get his ass to the shoulder quick enough. Full of the wrath that comes of being a superprivileged white man, and fighting off a concomitant anxiety that often becomes murderous panic, they will drive right over you, as if you were an empty junker in some coliseum and they the star of the Monster Truck Show.

My cat was sixteen years old at the time of our flight. She detested all forms of travel and would according to her tradition defecate after about five minutes in the car. I came to understand after a few years of this that the shit was being scared out of her. (One time, in Minneapolis, I think she decided she would rather die than stay in the car another second. Stopped in a rush-hour traffic jam near Lake Calhoun, I was annoyed to hear insistent horn-honking behind me. I looked in the rearview mirror and saw what I took to be a really impatient asshole laying on the thing and waving his arms. The lane next to us had begun to move and was suddenly moving quite swiftly.

The lane on the other side, too. Then we began to move. It was at this point that I saw my cat's hind paws disappear through the narrow band of space at the top of the window. She landed on the road at about the same time I did. I moved so fast I nearly caught her as she fell. Before either of us knew what had happened, we were back in the car and rocketing down Lake Street. I was so glad I hadn't flipped the guy off behind me, very pleased with the restraint I had luckily, that time, been able to exercise.)

It was three in the morning. There were no mountain men about, but the hairpin turns and the rising and falling of the road over the top of the mountains unsettled my cat even further, no matter how slowly I drove, no matter how gently I negotiated the bend. She took her first shit and I thought, as I scooped it up and tossed it into the bushes, that was that. She hadn't used her cat box, which was not a good sign, but at least it was over. I'd had the foresight to bring along a roll of paper towels and lots of water, so cleanup was a matter of a few seconds, and we were on our way.

Her second shit was diarrheic. We were maybe ten minutes into the journey now. I stopped and spent another ten minutes cleaning up the passenger seat. She got down into the cavelike foot well and I thought prepared to resign herself to those things over which she had no control. She began to pee just as I made a sharp turn that rolled her over. She rolled in the puddle and continued peeing as she rolled. She got to her feet and before I could stop we went around another sharp curve, tipping her over and rolling her back the other way.

I soaked up the urine and cleaned her fur as well as I could.

About a half hour in, she began to vomit. I stopped and cleaned it up. The second time she started to heave, I kept driving while ripping off a sheet of towel, holding it under her mouth as she vomited, and tossing it out the window. Go right on ahead, I thought, with your upchucking and what have you, I got this down and we're not stopping again 'til we reach Minnesota.

Dizzily, full of fear and nausea, she climbed over the seat back and vomited on my dog, who was fifteen years old and too weary to get out of the way, too weary to care. I stopped and cleaned everybody up. When I began to sob, I knew all was not so well with me as I'd hoped—or pretended, an actor for better or worse, to the bitter end—in the cool first imaginings I'd had of our escape.

We moved from Redlands to Forest Falls because we thought it would be cleaner, cooler, darker, quieter. We figured our neighbors would be kooky or hermitlike, but tolerant of, well, I was going to say eccentricity, but that's not it . . . tolerant of things that our neighbors in Redlands hadn't been tolerant of: an unsightly car parked on driveway (not in garage, where even sightly cars are supposed to rest), a dog too large for condo rules (they had one of those things you see in airports: CAN YOUR DOG FIT IN THIS?), not shutting the jets off in the hot tub immediately upon exit but letting them run an extra minute until the timer shut them off—things like that. Our Redlands neighbors sat in their houses and observed our every move. Everybody had a score pad. They were out to get us because we were *rent-ers*. One old woman who wanted to buy the place from our landlord came over often with a tape measure and a spiral-bound notebook. It was she who first told us of the immensity of our dog and the bylaws stacked against her. She was visibly relieved when she learned how old our dog was: *won't be a problem for long.*

We threw (literally, I threw) our nutty assortment of broken-down and useless belongings in a rented truck and I floored it up the mountain. So many people glared or gestured angrily at me that I became indifferent to it: *Doin' the best ah can, I sang, in mah movin' van!*

No, no, wait, I'm sorry: that's the image I have, the image I still have, of myself, buried deep in a smoking crevice of my brain. The truth was I was hanging out the window shouting all kinds of angry observations and instructions.

We crept up the narrow road to the cabin we'd rented. I backed the huge truck up the steep and narrow driveway. I threw things out of the truck. It was cool and clean and quiet. If it was true that we could stand inside our cabin and shake hands with our neighbors inside their cabins, it was also true that they were quiet. They were very quiet, but given, I learned, to spontaneous combustion. There is a condition called "canyon mentality," which is an effect of living atop one another in the narrow and sometimes gloomy confines of a canyon. Residents of other San Bernardino mountain communities tended to think of Forest Falls as a hotbed of sociopathy. There were, however, large numbers of reasonable and friendly people, too, there for the clean and the cool and the quiet. I tried to ingratiate myself with them by imitating them. Leslie passed without breaking a sweat.

The fourth day in our new home was the Fourth of July. We walked a quarter mile down the road to where the general store, the sheriff's satellite station, the Mexican restaurant, and the realty office were located. The great Forest Falls chili cook-off was in progress! I was in the throes of what turned out to be chronic dyspepsia and had misplaced my sunglasses, so there I was, squinting and grimacing and wondering if the guys dressed up like Hell's Angels lived in the area or were just visiting for the chili. A parade of pets passed by, and some children next to me jeered at the smaller or more nervous animals. A cat came by, on a leash held by a little girl in a pinafore, and they hollered with delight: IT'S A FUCKIN' CAT! One of them picked up a stone and I knocked him flat. He started to get up and I stepped on him. He started to cry and shout and I told him to shut the fuck up or I'd start breaking his bones.

No, no, wait, I'm sorry: that's the image I had, still have, of myself, buried deep in a smoking crevice of my brain.

We tried mouthfuls of the various chilis. The last one was called "All American Chili" or something like that. The big sign over the booth featured a flag and a warning that the chili was harmful to gays, liberals, and the residents of every country of Central and South America— all of which were listed. There were some other groups included, blacks, Jews, and so on. What have you. All in good fun, I thought, ha ha! JESUS LOVES YOU! YOU GOT A PROBLEM WITH THAT? Even white supremacist militia men take golfing holidays! One fella's big truck sported a bumper sticker that suggested he was ready and willing to shove the cell phones of inattentive drivers up their asses. He had his cell wedged between cheek and shoulder as he backed over a garbage can full of chili cups. He was saying how he was in his truck, he had a cell phone and he was in his truck, yeah, yeah, he nodded as he gunned his way out of the garbage can and the phone slipped free, tangling in his beard. Disentangling it, he excitedly told his friend he had driven over a garbage can and was now backing out of it. "Don't eat the tourist, Rex," he cautioned the dog.

On the 11th of July, after two days of on-and-off rain (about a half inch), a monstrous storm cell developed over San Gorgonio. It rained hard that morning and lightning struck all around our cabin. Leslie was in San Diego (she was already in flight, but her cover story was that she was visiting her brother and our nephews), and while I spoke to her on the phone, the strikes were so loud that she thought something terrible was happening. I told her it was only raining. The sky was viridian green with all the electrical discharge going on, but darkening as if the descent of night took minutes and not hours. The strokes of lightning were like seams of white blood against the black sky. When they struck, the house shook. Streams of sediment boiled down the roads.

I left. I was one of the last people to get out. Two inches of rain—three in some spots, according to the

Doppler data—fell in about an hour. Down one of the three principal drainages in the Forest Falls area, the Snow Creek drainage, came fifty million gallons of water carrying mud, trees, boulders—and, once it hit houses—houses and people. Fifteen homes were destroyed, one woman was killed—suffocated in mud in her living room while her mother was carried off down the mountain, bones breaking one after the other until she came to rest in a kind of backwater of shrubs and mud. Another woman, quite old, was buried up to her neck for three hours. Power was out for a day, water for five. For nearly two days I did not know if our cabin was still there, our dog and our cat still alive. It seemed unlikely, as people who could come down came down and told us what had happened. My road was in the heart of the worst-hit area, but what I think happened was that the mud slide split more or less in two, the main stream going down the big road and a little tongue of it through my backyard. The houses on our road were situated on a kind of island, it seemed, and had been spared.

I could not sleep after the mud slide. My personality is nerve-racked on the best of days, all signs and figures ominous but impenetrably obscure, dread settling upon me like graveyard fog, through which I whistle—and it just got worse. Couldn't whistle. Could hardly speak. Tongue like lead, lips as if shot through with Novocain. Still, there were moments of delight. The first two days after the slide we spent in a luxury suite high atop the San Diego resort where my brother-in-law is chef of all chefs.

A wildfire broke out on the hillside on the other side of the highway. Like soldiers in a foxhole, we sighed: it was the other guy's resort that got it. My dog's bladder and legs were growing weaker by the day, the only grass was not only ten flights down but across the highway, burning up—and of course dogs were not allowed in the resort. In the first place. Squatting in Forest Falls had been a trial: with no flat surfaces anywhere, she sometimes tipped over, unless I was holding her. I know what many of you are thinking: this was clearly a dog at the end of her days. The thought that I would have to put her down was in fact the only articulate thought I could make out in the whine and babble of my head, a simple refrain I could see coming and going at all times as its turn came and went around in the terrible music of fear. But her eyes were clear and bright, her appetite—a trademark— still overwhelming, her tail wagged and I could see no signs of the pain I'd seen in other old dogs. I massaged her and she calmed me. I sometimes think now that she was holding on just to see me through a bad time. But back to the luxury suite: she wandered out onto the balcony and took a long, satisfying pee on that spacious flat surface. It spattered and pooled and then began to spread. I grabbed newspapers and slapped them down on the river just as it reached the edge of the balcony. Perhaps a drop or two fell on the table ten floors below, poolside. Or on the bald head of the man sitting at the table, drinking a tall drink, poolside. If they did, he did not remark it, did not look up, did not see the boy and his dog grinning down at him.

2

We arrived in Barstow at dawn. It was ninety-five already. Everybody in the convenience store where I gassed up seemed tense and irritable, as if some kind of burglary were taking place and I was being allowed to pass in and out of it. Some hapless millionaire nitwit on the blaring TV pointed mirthlessly at a map of the United States and chuckled. It was all red. It would be over a hundred all the way to Minnesota. In Pierre, South Dakota, the day before, it had reached 111. Baseball scores came on and the clerk swore violently. He told everybody how much he hated baseball. It was too slow. Somebody laughed, but the clerk just shook his head, genuinely angry as far as I could tell.

First night, Gallup, New Mexico. I'd been driving for four-teen hours, looking in the back seat every five minutes or so to see if dog or cat had died. The motel was cheap but I would nevertheless pay dearly. My dog shit on the sidewalk and I scraped it up, put it down the toilet, and moved on to the cat shit on the bed. Cleaned that up, put it down the toilet, flushed it, left the bathroom, heard water spilling, rushed back in to see toilet overflowing. Bought nondescript fast food and a can of beer too big to hold comfortably in one hand. Tried to sleep but could not. The TV was blaring in the next room just as it had in the Barstow convenience store—the only difference was a laugh track. I was dazed and weak enough not to care, but around midnight I called the front desk to complain:

no answer. Went to front desk: no one there. Returned to room and banged on wall. Called up room next door: no answer. Let phone ring and ring and ring. Then, as it rang, went out and banged on door: dead or extremely indifferent. Around three I heard the occupants return: ha ha ha, we left the TV on! Nothing could have been funnier to these folks, because they laughed and laughed and laughed.

Dusk of day two found us not yet out of New Mexico, which was extremely discouraging. We were close, in the town of Raton, and the mountains seemed remarkably more hospitable: broad, beflowered meadows through which the little Escort motored easily. After hours in passing gear but going no faster than fifty, the temp needle creeping past the L of NORMAL, this was a great relief. We were way up and it was cooler, but flatter. I spoke enthusiastically of these differences to dog and cat. I reminded them of the late great comedian Bill Hicks's bit about Arizona Bay: California after the Big One, and how we were free. I reminded them of the line in *Monty Python and the Holy Grail*: "Not dead yet!" But rooms were hard to come by in Raton that day: a Little League tournament or something like that was taking place. I mumbled, turned away a third time, that children should not be traveling about the country in order to play. And when I found myself in the pet food aisle of a vast, cold grocery store, I could not help but weep. Luckily the nearest customers were at the other end of the aisle, about fifty yards off, and must have thought I was sneezing.

Room was found for us at the fourth inn, though I was forced to deny my dog and cat. As I hustled them furtively in I pondered deeply in myself and asked was it indeed not shameful so to have denied them? It was. I stepped outside and shouted, "I have a dog and a cat!"

I drank half a pint of whiskey but failed to feel even the good old loosening of the limbs that was the first sign of happy, deepening drunkenness. My dog went to the door sometime in the middle of the night and began to pee. I leapt, literally leapt, and dove under her with a towel. Sometime later, I heard the cat vomit, followed, minutes later, by the dog.

I washed several towels in the motel's laundry and took a long hot shower. Refreshed, but technically drunk, I left the maid a ten-dollar bill and a note saying I was sorry, and departed in the dreaminess of the first murmur of dawn.

Somewhere east of Denver a highway cop floated past me in the oncoming lane, gesturing threateningly but vaguely. I shrugged theatrically, taking both hands off the wheel, slowed, and pulled over, but he just kept on going. "Fare thee well, nymph!" I called out in my best Ian Richardson imitation. Something like that. Certainly not what I said to the Chicago cop, a certain something that had angered him unreasonably and which put my liberty in jeopardy. But that was years earlier. Or months?

Somewhere near the Kansas and Nebraska border, a great feeling of peace overcame me, unmistakably like the feeling

I had when I swam out too far in Lake Superior and became too cold to swim back. At first I attributed it to the
level ground, the empty road (I could count on one hand
the cars I'd passed in an hour), the outermost pales of the
homeland, but the sense of reverie acted on me like a nar-
cotic, and I found it increasingly difficult to drive.

I felt weak, tired, and cold. I stopped the car and
rolled down my window. The ovenlike heat was strangely
but powerfully consoling. I shuddered, then wept in a
way I can only describe as reflexively, as if an invisible
physician had tapped my heartspring with a mallet. The
idea that I might not go further did not trouble me. I was
instantly asleep but slept for no more than five minutes,
during which successive shadows passed over me and the
car shook violently. When I awoke the sky looked yellow,
then gray, then blue. The engine was still ticking. I had no
idea where we were and no desire to know. Dusty rows of
corn twelve feet high rustled faintly. A tractor-trailer rig
passed like a great wind of redemption. The car darkened
and shook for a second, then all was quiet again. There
was a deep, abiding smell of manure drifting through the
car. I wiped the sweat from my face with a long, elaborate
gesture—more a massage of facial muscles or an explora-
tion of the outer casing of a mysterious engine of pain
shut down without warning or apparent cause, a little
ominously as the seconds ticked past, in the middle of a
fantastic nowhere.

I carried my dog from the car to the edge of the ditch.
We stood there for a while as if hypnotized, staring at the
corn. I say hypnotized but there was no sense of a cloud

of unknowing. The narcotic-like swoon had been refined and clarified and was now a kind of headless tranquility. I like to think, now, long after the fact, that my dog and I saw the corn, smelled the manure, heard the birds, felt the hot, dry dirt on the same level of perception, with the same kind of perception. And I see now that that was the moment when I knew we had successfully fled California.

I think of anxiety, of nervous dread, as fear for which there can be no appeal, no relief—because it is baseless, sourceless, amorphous, omnipresent. It is the kind of fear, to paraphrase Montaigne, that dreads even help. One cannot imagine or remember calmer, happier times: it is a present from which all the juice and joy of sensual life has been sucked. A desert island in an ocean of formaldehyde, on which one crouches in the shade of a plastic palm tree. It's very like stage fright: the actor alone in a hot, bright spotlight, unable to remember lines, the carefully constructed biography, the analogs of emotion, the gestures and signs—and unable to imagine any consequence other than unending heart-pounding fear: no return of gesture from a fellow actor, no reply to line, no encouragement from the audience in the dark, no laughter or breathless silence, no applause.

California is a state of high anxiety, and it lies everywhere upon the earth. Like Montaigne's "black care," it squats behind the parting horseman, troll hands resting lightly on the rider's shoulders.

I had driven until I could drive no more, the border always retreating before me like a mirage, and when I stopped, it was gone.

3

The little Escort that could underwent a mysterious break-down and repair, too, at another dawn, somewhere in the Sand Hills. We went up and down several small but steep hills in quick succession—much more like a roller-coaster ride than Cal 38 through the San Bernardinos had been, and going down the last one, the transmission dropped into second and wouldn't shift back up.

I decided to continue on, even though the engine was now revving at twice the speed it had been revving to maintain something close to highway velocity. This may sound reckless and foolhardy, but that is my way. Something happened to a car I was driving in eastern Pennsylvania—a seal blew, I think, I don't really know; all I knew was that I had to floor it to keep my speed up, literally keep the pedal on the floor. And so I did. I could see the gas gauge needle dropping and I must have gassed up five or six times before I got to my home in Connecticut. But I got there.

Roaring up and down the rest of the Sand Hills, I came to a service station. I carried dog and cat from the car and sat them down at a picnic table up to its benches in dewy grass. We wandered about in a humming jittery daze for a few moments while the tank was being filled. Then I paid for the gas and a breakfast bar, or power bar, or something not quite a candy bar but very like a candy bar. And a cup of coffee. (My rule was to never leave a place where I'd stopped without a cup of coffee.) I put everybody back in the car and pulled out onto the highway, where I was delighted to hear the engine rev and the transmission shift from first to second to third. Would the mysterious drop and lock into second happen again? I didn't care, because I understood the ritual now: stop car, turn it off, turn it on again, proceed. It might take another day to get to Minnesota, but this seemed a trivial, petty consideration. The main thing was to keep going.

We finally did arrive at my mother's home in a suburb of Minneapolis. It was late afternoon, and we all fell asleep less than an hour later. I slept for sixteen hours, and when I awoke my dog had raised her head from her pillow. She wagged her tail and grinned her panting grin at me. She slowly eased herself up from the pillow and we walked into the backyard. We looked around at the cottonwood trees and my old rusting motorcycle very much as we had looked at the cornfield. She peed, then leaned up against the house and looked up at me. I carried her inside and she died.

My wife's flight from San Francisco arrived later that day. She saw from a very great distance that Woody had died. There. I named her. She was part of a litter of barely weaned puppies my neighbor had found in a box on the side of a road in 1984. We kept them all in the fenced backyard and unused garage of the house where I was living then, and we named them just to keep them straight. One of them had a wood tick on her half the size of her body. Though she was a female, I said, "We'll call this one Woody!"

She was cremated and we buried her ashes on Madeline Island in Lake Superior. The sky that day was divided between storm and infinite blue. To the east it was black as night, but the sun in the west lit everything up that lay before the darkness with that numinous quality that comes only of starkest contrast, good and evil, night and day. The lake and boulders of the shore and the docks and cabins and the quaking and the balsam fir all glowed against the black curtain. Like props on an immense stage. Leslie called out to me. I could barely hear her over the crash of the waves on the shore, but I looked up just in time to see three white birds, lit so brilliantly I could see their eyes, the lines of individual feathers, their yellow beaks open and close, hovering for a second in the wind, veering, then gone.

I dreamt that night of a golden dog crossing a road.

the
barber-chair

The sky was as blue as if all of space were blue, as if the outer darkness and all its unimaginably remote crystalline spheres and slowly revolving heavenly bodies were shades of blue. Thirty big dogs had drilled holes in the snow with hot jets of urine. All around me the snow had yellowed. Here and there large turds smoked and froze in form-fitting troughs of snow. My big, warm boots crunched the squeaking snow, a sensation and sound I have always found pleasant, even soothing. It seemed nothing would give way: my footing was sure and easy, and the wind blew heavily, slowly, quietly—like a mighty orchestra in some oceanic largo of death—through the trees sheltering my cabin. I looked up at the sky: it didn't seem real. Had something happened to the universe that the sky should no longer seem real? Had something happened to me?

Was something about to happen? It dizzied and troubled me, this deep, lovely blue, in a way the night sky or a sky of storm never could, and I dropped my gaze.

It was a warm day, no more than a few degrees below the Fahrenheit zero. Several weeks had passed with the thermometer moving imperceptibly upward from thirty below and imperceptibly back, so the sudden leap to zero made me feel almost clammy—faintly nervous and faintly nauseous. The longer I stood in the bright sunlight, the hotter my head felt, as if lasers were boring into my brain through my eyes and cooking it. My dogs sounded like vicious, maddened junkyard killers. The steam of neurotic concern came out my ears, but as I poured white-fish stew into their bowls and watched them lap and chew and swallow, my head cooled and drained. The steam of the broth and the clouds of our breath rose like fog and burned off in the blue. I felt tall, taller, taller still, gigantic standing on the iron crust of the deep snow. The barking grew fainter and less harsh, until at last the dogs sounded nearly human.

The sky was merely blue. The trees were black and green as if painted with lacquer. Around a tiny brown cabin dug into a hillside, rocks and boulders exposed by the wind were glittering gray and lichen green. Everything else was white. The lake was two thousand feet deep and the cliffs of its islands rose up like sentient things the minutes of whose lives were as millennia to us. They seemed to stare back at me as if I had suddenly appeared within the spectrum of size and light they could perceive. The North Pole was very near. It was like a magical tropical paradise just visible in the distance, or an approaching storm, a silver luminescence low in the northern sky darkening at the horizon to a black, brilliant seam of light separating two worlds.

Antonia watched me hook roaring dogs to my sled in that careful, vigilant, penetrating way that was peculiarly hers—as if everything—everything—depended on my not making even a small mistake. Small mistakes were in fact the worst—precisely because they were so easy to overlook. Antonia was small and lean and hard, a ropey-muscled rock climber, filthy rich. When I was done and my team fell silent, hers commenced a thunderous fugue up and down the line. It was as if they were rival camps who taunted each other according to ancient ritual, feigning a jubilant contempt, grinning and yapping the old insults. They took no notice of the too blue sky, which Antonia remarked as I had. She recalled for me a description of a surrealist production of a play by Apollinaire, *Les mamelles de Tiresias*: the naughty surrealists had kept the audience waiting for two hours, staring at a curtain "so blue it was offensive." Her mother, Betty, was a scholar who had written extensively on the Surrealists; her father, Ralph, dead twenty years, had sat on boards and played in a string quartet characterized by many rolling bottles of claret, immense smoking cigars, and loud, laughing disagreements. That anyway was how she remembered it—but of her childhood generally, little else.

When she was done, the dogs had lapsed into what passed among them for repose. We had two strong, balanced, complete teams, several retired dogs, and more pups than I cared to count. Our lead dogs were incomparably virtuous, invincible animals—Maeve, who could hypnotize everybody she looked at, and Luther, given to fits of awful insight—and the following twenty-eight were insanely strong, relentless, and optimistic. We happily agreed we could go anywhere and do anything with them: transport enthusiasts of endangered species east to the Thelon Sanctuary, and mountain climbers west to Nahanni and the Cirque of the Unclimbables—a thousand miles would be nothing to them. We would stop flying people around and mush them instead. Get the really big spenders with time on their hands and away we'd go. We could win the Iditarod five years in a row and that would be our calling card. The dogs seemed to want to do everything they could to make our dreams come true. They seemed to want nothing more than to eat, shit, fuck, sleep, pull sleds, and make our dreams come true. Left to their own devices, some turned into tormenting bullies, some into vicious fighters, but one of the great pleasures of my life has been to wade into dogfights and break them up. Padded and protected like a police trainer in my everyday gear, I feel them slamming into me, sometimes knocking me to the ground, getting on top of me and staring deeply into my eyes, calming down, wagging tails, licking and whining.

I called out the command to march, heard Antonia's echo, muffled by her face mask, and they began to move. We walked behind the sleds for a few paces then ran, the squeaking of our boots quickly lost once we were beyond the sheltering trees and down onto the lake, lost in the wind and the rasp of the runners in the hard snow and the steady jingling and rush of smoking white air in and out of thirty dogs. We picked up speed and our troubles eased. In the cold, cold wind, under the ominous blue bow of heaven, the dogs ran faster and faster. We had never known them to run so fast. It was thrilling. The lake had taken forever to freeze that fall, but now we were free.

Four months later we were in San Diego and behaving with slightly exaggerated good manners toward each other. Spring Santa Anas came in off the desert and it was so hot I had trouble breathing. We had a suite in the Marriott, on the twenty-third floor of a building shaped like the prow of an immense mirrored ocean liner. A hugely successful manufacturer of software was holding its annual conference there, and we sat in the cafes and bars or at the pool just outside the flow of ten thousand bustling, cheerful workers, vendors, and business partners. They all wore large plastic-coated name and admittance tags around their necks—which the Santa Anas and ocean breezes would catch, lift, and spin as their wearers walked from hotel to convention center, or along the marina to Seaport Village for lunch. No one seemed drunken or lecherous in the old way of conventions, and if the necklaces of the spinning ID tags seemed to wind, like the rubber band of a toy airplane, threateningly closer and closer to the necks around which they were hung, neither of us could help but feel that we were being woven willy-nilly back into the sturdy and colorful fabric of a great civilization we had thought to do without.

But it seemed, too, a dream. The expansive view from the room, high above so much life and industry, the high white arc of the Coronado Bridge over the blue Pacific, the foamy lines far below of the wakes of huge yachts diverging, disappearing, U.S. Navy ships and helicopters coming and going almost silently on the other side of the glass, the freight trains and trolleys cityside, the crowns of palm trees heaving in the hot, dry wind—even the ice melting in the bucket seemed odd, an isolated incident, terrible in the way it suggested the truth lay in such transformations—only seeming to shimmer just below the surface, ready to emerge in an unlooked-for moment, after a lapse of time, a period of decay, a mistake in judgment.

I looked at the mirrored panels of the balconies of the hotel's north tower. The sailboats and party yachts of the marina were reflected almost perfectly, as if it were a gigantic mural. When a helicopter appeared in one panel, I touched Antonia's arm. Together we watched as the image of the helicopter moved from one balcony to the next. When it was gone, Antonia sighed and turned away. I turned and stared into the empty sky whence it had come. Antonia began to weep. She had wept before, and always with good reason. I suppose, at that point, I admired or even envied, with a cool, remote kind of appraising envy, her capacity to weep. She would weep and she would have me fly her south and she would be gone for a month, two months, then come back stronger than ever. It was perhaps the only way she could remain vigilant. That night we concluded the sale of our plane, an old, immaculate Grumman Widgeon, to a group of well-to-do environmentalists whom we suspected planned to use it in bombing raids on whaling ships. Walking away, I felt numb and

confused. It was true that Norway and Japan were exert-
ing pressure on the international whaling community to
lift the ban, and looked to have their way, but I wondered
in the crowded, noisy lobby of the hotel if it wasn't whale
watchers who were to be targeted. I asked Antonia, and
she said something about asking Alexander Cockburn because what did she know, she knew nothing, and I nodded
vacantly at the apparent truth of it, the bitter strength of
her conviction. She had continued her weeping more or
less all day. I did not want my plane to be used in that way,
in either way. I wanted it to loft people blissfully into the
air—nervous, frightened people, despairing people, tired,
empty people for whom life on Earth was a torment—
and bring them gently back down to a new world, because
everything, I thought I saw quite clearly now, hung in the
balance of experienced judgment and moderate responses
to clamorous stimuli. People had to be treated carefully
but powerfully. And if I couldn't fly my plane in this way,
I wanted to think that someone would.

The next day we were in Chicago, where we saw a couple
we hadn't seen since our wedding two years earlier. After
a night of embarrassingly frank revelations from Conrad
and Shelly (they were unhappy), which seemed to preempt
all the things we needed to say as well as short-circuit
Antonia's weeping, we continued our flight to Connecticut,
where her family had lived for centuries.

The weeping intensified and became without warning angry jabs at her sister, brother, mother, husband. It was as

if she were asleep when crying and, startled awake, rudely, roughly roused from dreams of such bitter reproach she could not clear them from her mind.

The quarrels were conducted mainly in a peevish and irritable manner, over inconsequential things, or sarcastically, as if joking, over grievances from childhood. Elizabeth, for instance, a reporter for a Hartford television station, was an easygoing, good-natured woman given secretly to vice of all kinds, who had never, as a child, been caught in the performance of her many sins, and who, consequently (Antonia believed), had taken on a superior, condescending air toward people who had been caught at something and who now required forbearance and forgiveness. Sometimes it came in handy—forgiveness, after all, was forgiveness—but Toni was tired of it. *Thanks for all the forgiveness,* she said, *I really couldn't eat another bite!* Patrick, her brother, a sculptor enjoying sudden and amazing popularity, whose "animals" were being installed, one after another, around the world, left his house a jam-packed and filthy mess on purpose, to keep people from being comfortable and thus, eventually, from coming over at all. He was secretive and unfriendly and she was tired of it. His work, too, she said to me, struck her as banal. And his wife, Suzanne! The rosy smugness of her pregnancy made Antonia want to slap her. Her mother, Toni whispered angrily, lacked the moral gentleness of her father, making it impossible for Antonia to feel that her life of complicated trials and errors had ever been acceptable. She had always felt that way, and she was officially sick and tired of it. And me, whose quiet, shy intelligence—

her words—had seemed such perfect purgative to the casual arrogance and educated ignorance—her words—of her friends, I now became a misanthrope, a willful and frightened man—her words—whose wish to live in the middle of nowhere was an example of looking for trouble in its purest form. Counting the daughters of Rose and William Styron among her best friends, she consequently had the Styrons' guesthouse on Martha's Vineyard—the house that depression built, the author liked to say, referring to his popular memoir of suicidal misery—to escape to, and did so, without a word to anyone in the family.

I thought my brother-in-law's sculptures were extraordinarily beautiful. The ostriches particularly please me. A pair of them, life-size, flanked the gated entrance to an ostrich farm in Simsbury. A herd of bison, also life-size, six of them, decorated the lawn of Citibank's operation in South Dakota. He'd recently traveled to Thailand to install some water buffalo. He was working on a parade of elephants for a restaurant in Los Angeles while employing numerous friends, who put together wire-and-wood frames for the birds and fish and small woodland creatures that sold in the hundreds. They gathered in the soft light filtering down through the skylights in his remodeled barn, smoked a lot of pot, and whistled while they worked. Most of them were gypsy carpenters as well, and had helped him build his house and several outbuildings. If they played music it was Hank Snow and Ernest Tubb and Kitty Wells or Thelonious Monk or show tunes: "Seventy-six Trombones" or "Can Do." There was an old trailer home sinking into the weeds at the far edge of the cleared land, and it was his idea that I should live there until Antonia came back. He did not believe Antonia was coming back, and was frank enough in the revelation of this belief—her time in the Northwest Territories had been the aberrant dalliance of a rich Amazon—but used a code for the sake of easy conversation with me. He liked me as much as I liked him, I think, and was not arrogant. That Antonia had come and gone but mostly come for almost a decade seemed not to register: time was not the salient measure. Neither was devotion, which was merely a function of time. They were rich and I didn't understand. *She's done all she can for you,* he told me sarcastically. His compound was spread out in a little meadow, on a foothill of the Berkshires, and the trailer was higher up than his house, though with an occluded view. The land sloped up sharply behind it, maybe another five hundred feet. It was a steep but easy climb that I made every day—not so much in atonement or humble hope as in restless despair; I desired to live simply and do good deeds with no reference to time or devotion but rather to frustration and fatigue. Antonia would come back, and I would be forgiven, or not. There was nothing I could do. In the end it made me feel humble. Maybe it was mock-humble. I don't know. Nor am I sure I wanted Antonia back.

A couple of weeks passed. Antonia departed the Vineyard for New York, but I didn't try to find her. Eventually she called, leaving a message that informed me she didn't want to talk. I assumed the role of bailiff on Patrick's estate and slept outside most nights, with his dogs. I saw to his orchards and began rebuilding the three-hundred-year-old stone fence that rose and fell across his land. He wanted to grade his steep and winding drive, and cut runoff channels here and there along its length, so I fired up his front-end loader and familiarized myself with its levers.

One day, after bringing up a load of gravel in his dump truck, he said that he had been finished with our wedding present for some time. His plan was to give it to me if Antonia couldn't get her shit together. I assumed it was a piece of sculpture and said he should donate it to a school. We got out of the truck and one of his friends hailed us from the door of the bird factory. It was somebody Patrick wanted to talk to, calling on the telephone. He jogged off. The friend shouted again and I turned to see the truck moving backward about the distance of one revolution of its big wheels.

We had neglected to set the parking brake. The truck moved another wheel's worth backward. The ground we were on was relatively level, but if it kept going it would quickly reach a steeper slope, which would send it hurtling down the hill and into a ravine. I stepped behind it, slapped my hands against the gate, and braced my legs. The truck continued its slow roll. I locked my arms and dug my heels in. The truck picked up speed. I understood that I was an irredeemable fool as my boots slipped in the hard-packed dirt and gravel. Cocked at a heroic forty-five-degree angle to the truck, I began to slide backward with it. Patrick's friend was now on the running board and hauling himself in through the window—as the driver-side door had been dented and could not be opened. I went down and the truck rolled over me. The friend jammed on the brakes just before it reached the slope. I lay there in the warm sunlight just long enough to feel the wind ruffle my hair, and then I stood up.

That weekend a gallery owner threw a party. In deep New England spring twilight I sat down at a picnic table with a plate of food and looked up to see Arthur Miller sitting across from me. I swallowed my food and told the internationally famous playwright I had once played Biff, in a college production. He nodded as if surprised and I went on to describe it as one of the great moments of my life. He nodded again and said it was a good part for a young man.

Elizabeth was one of the celebrity hosts at a golf tournament going on that weekend, and her camera crew had caught her teeing off and shanking one viciously into the trees. Because her public personality was one of immense dignity, the news director ran the footage, which included a cut to Elizabeth visibly but not audibly cursing. I walked with her for a while amongst the heaped and rusting girders, gigantic tableware, and mysterious turds of contemporary sculpture, the rowboat tipped up on its bow, the teeter-totter running on a small electric motor with two lifelike children rising and falling all night long, and listened to her field jokes about her game. Then a young, sleek man came up and said he watched her all the time, to which she replied she hoped he meant on TV, and we all laughed.

The taller sculptures were now black and ominous against a dark gray sky in which the last of the evening's light was glowing, a fading flare that caused certain colors in people's clothing to stand out luminously while their hands and arms and faces disappeared in the cool humid murk of night.

A white dress appeared before me. The woman wearing it spoke and I recognized her as an old friend of Patrick's wife. I thought her name was Lisa but I stopped just short of saying it, in a sudden and remarkably violent moment of doubt. There were large numbers of dancers present—some Martha Clarke people, some Pilobolus and Momix people, a handful of international stars—and I had the impression Lisa danced or had danced, but of this too I was very likely visibly uncertain. Lisa named herself and continued talking to me as if I were a nervous horse. Her tone was comforting and friendly, almost motherly as she went on, even grandmotherly at times, telling me how often and how admiringly Patrick spoke of me. At some point in the murmuring it came to me that she administered Patrick's business dealings. She slipped her hand under my arm and steered me like an investment through the appreciative crowd: I was suddenly the envy of everybody on the lawn. It wasn't until several months after the events of the next day that I understood the assumptions people were making, the rumors that were instantly abroad, that this dreamily beautiful, kind, intelligent woman had dropped her longtime lover—Patrick— and taken up with me, Jack London. One camp chalked it up to a combination of changes in Patrick's character wrought by impending fatherhood and the mysterious allure of the Arctic that I embodied. Another camp had the mysterious allure, but with Antonia's nascent lesbianism somehow figuring. The third had Lisa infamously bored, as Antonia had been before she met me, willing to give a brooding misfit the benefit of the doubt, with special attention to the mysterious allure. It was all absurd: Lisa never had the slightest intention of leaving New York, and what everybody failed to consider was my desire to return, which did not in fact exist, at that point, either.

I did end up talking a great deal. I suppose I was beginning to think it was safe to speak. Or rather, that Lisa began to make me feel that it was safe to speak. Perhaps it was a consequence of Antonia's continuing absence. I'd received a card from Martha's Vineyard: *It's really really nice here. I am tired but everyone is great about leaving me alone.* Lisa's white dress became less vivid and her voice merely a murmur, every now and then, of encouragement. We slapped a few mosquitoes but of course their size and number were insignificant compared to common experience in the Northwest Territories. Patrick joined us, asking leading questions cleverly designed to make me larger than life, my anecdotes exemplary. I felt like a common fraud but wanted ardently to deceive Lisa as to my character. I spoke of the "scenic wonders" of the South Nahanni's canyons, its waterfall—twice the height of Niagara—and the "outstanding hydraulics" of the run itself. I spoke about green silty water roaring over boulders, making them bright and glassy, and the faces of box canyon walls three thousand feet straight up painted yellow and orange by rusting iron. I said that the river was an excellent example of "antecedence," in that it was older than the north-south-running ranges it bisected—the Caribou, the Headless, and the Funeral. As talk of mountains seemed to please her, I described the Raggeds, the already-mentioned Cirque, the Parrot's Beak, and the Lotus Flower Tower, a "big wall" climb I had made with Antonia leading: Class 5, A2, V, golden granite with a long crack hanging like a thread, from summit to base, lots of rope management, chock and piton use relatively easy, with a bivouac ledge out of a fable, a few square feet of meadow floating like a magic carpet in the sky. She asked about the business and I described the enthusiasts of endangered species we flew to the Barren Grounds, the bird-watchers to Wood Buffalo for crane, whitewater people to Moose Ponds on the upper river where it drops thirty feet every mile, or to the Flat with its Class VI water and the Cascade-of-the-Thirteen-Steps. We took some anglers to the Prairie Creek for the Dolly Varden and we took daytrippers and over-nighters to the campgrounds by the falls. I flew so much I got my instrument rating and my commercial ticket almost overnight. Years, however, were beginning to pass. We took hikers to hot springs that had overflowed the rims of their pools, calcified and flowed, calcified and flowed, un-til the springs were giant mushroom caps of tufa, stepped domes with tiny concave baths and fountains atop them. Or to Chinook trap gardens of Eden where (Antonia and I averred, drawling and grinning and winking around our com mikes like good old boy fighter pilots) snow never fell because it stayed warm all the subarctic winter long, and "the place of the live winds," where one traversed a landscape of pink pillars, lime hoodoos, and aquamarine omegas. I told her how the name of the lake derived from a tribe called Slavey, who traded with the Goats in the Mackenzies and Selwyns, who in turn spoke of another tribe, "the people over there far away," seldom seen, not altogether human, ten feet tall, white men came to believe, headhunters, brain eaters—finding skeletons undisturbed by scavengers, but with heads removed some ten paces or so and cracked open—with horns as big as the equally rare Dall rams with whom their women lay. Lisa, I said, we flew a lot of dogs and dog people around, because there were lots of them around to fly, and because we were spending so much time with them, we came to resemble them.

"You know what," said Patrick, "nobody here really understands what happened to you and Toni up there. Why you came back and everything." He spoke with the breezy false confidentiality of someone who wanted to close a deal.

"That's because we don't like to talk about it." I laughed.

"Why don't you like to talk about it?" Patrick laughed.

"I made a stupid mistake." Lisa laughed like someone giving lines, in a rehearsal.

Arthur Miller passed and stopped to say goodnight to Lisa because it was impossible to resist stopping and talking to her. I told him I had also played Hap on alternate nights, which wasn't true. I just wanted Lisa to think of me as not simply an outdoorsman and bush pilot—however attractive that might have been—but Miller looked at me and then at Lisa with a look of very clear, very frank incredulity and dismay. It was as if I could have exhibited no greater weakness of character than to have lied so poorly, in a blatant attempt to impress a young woman, about my role in his play, his life. Lisa rose to kiss him and he went off mollified. I saw how she might remind him of Marilyn.

"Have you seen Patrick's present yet?"

"No," I said. "He said it was a secret."

"He's very uneasy about it."

Patrick demonstrated his unease by frowning.

"Do you want to see it?" he asked.

"Of course I do. I just don't think—"

"You really haven't seen it?"

"The door's locked. And there's a shade drawn over the window."

"Come with me." Lisa stood and took my hand. "I'll show you where the key is. There's this terrible momentum now, in the keeping of the secret. You know how he is. If you don't see it now you'll never see it. Never ever." Patrick frowned again and I felt his uneasiness settle around me.

Lisa drove in a way peculiar to northwestern Connecticut: as if she were on the Nurburgring in a Formula One car, up and down and around the narrow potholed off-camber roads, four-wheel drifting in perfect synchronicity with oncoming vehicles also four-wheel drifting. We hit the ramp up to Patrick's drive with a bang and a spray of gravel, and the beams of her headlights shot back and forth like a searchlight hooked up to a windshield-wiper motor. The dogs barked and scattered, leaping out of the way, then digging in for all they were worth in the race to beat us to wherever we were going. In the side mirror I saw them slamming on the brakes, wheeling, and coming after us. We shot past the barn and the house and the heavy-equipment shed, a couple of storage sheds, then slewed to a stop in a roar of gravel in front of a small building dug into the side of the hill, just across from my trailer. The key was under the mat.

The door we entered put us on a kind of mezzanine, a scaffolding running along three walls. We walked carefully the length of one wall, over cans of paint and sticky plaster, before we got to the light switch.

A huge piece lay under the blue tarp. It must have been fifty feet square, and under the tarp, its peaks and valleys suggested a model of mountains—which is what I guessed it was, a topo sculpture of the land in which we had lived, for so many years, so completely apart from family and friends. Lisa walked to the tarp and bent toward it, but stopped midreach, straightened, and looked back at Patrick and me. She looked uncertain to the point of fright. We looked at her for a moment in the fluorescent light.

"I don't know who I think I am to take such a liberty," she said.

"Lisa," said Patrick, partly a call of friendly comfort, partly a joking answer to her question. The doubt had come upon her so suddenly, so violently, and I knew her so superficially, that I wasn't sure what to say. It occurred to me that she was thinking of Toni. Patrick had a look on his face that everyone in the family wore when they were unhappily confused. Without looking at the sculpture, I tugged and folded the dusty tarp off to a corner, then turned to appraise it.

Patrick and Suzanne had come one summer to visit, and I remember him taking roll after roll of photographs; it was from one of those pictures that he had worked on the piece before us: thirty dogs, a roiling snarling laughing mass of fur and teeth, mounting each other, barking, howling at the moon, gazing serenely off into the distance. He had captured Maeve and Luther miraculously well: I thought I could almost look into their eyes and see them. He had managed arnica daisies—yellow in life—penstemons fruticosus, purple, islands of bluebells and blue delphiniums, lichen that had been orange and black, patches of tripe-de-roche, a bed of saxifrage and a carpet of bearberry, even a whiskey jack tucking a berry behind a curl of bark in the blasted trunk of a tree that rose up in the middle of the dogs.

There was a ringing in my ears and the sculpture seemed small and far off.

I lay with my head in Lisa's lap. The urge to kiss her, so overwhelming only an hour earlier, had faded and been forgotten. Beyond her head I could see stars. One shot fast and white across the sky so low it disappeared into the trees. Patrick was standing a few feet off, smoking a cigar.

We'd had a moose and whitefish winter—that was what the local Indians called a good winter—followed by a caribou winter, less good but not bad, followed by a starving-on-rabbits winter. We weren't starving, of course, but there was a feeling of desolation and remorselessness all around us, of stillness and the nearness of death. It seemed, to us both, unmistakably at times, that we had in fact already died and were ghosts, sitting on chairs in the dim light of our cabin, watching the luminous snow fall while the layers and layers of clothes we wore, the silk, the cotton, the wool, the down, rotted from our limbs. The lake was frozen solid half the year. We were often out on it. It was easier traveling than along the shore where there were thousand-foot climbs over boulders slick with ice. Legendarily, the narrows, called Tal-thel-ay, between the island nearest us, Oot-sing-gree-ay, and the mainland, were said never completely to freeze. A quarter of a mile wide, with a strong westerly current and the impassive faces of cliffs rising up on either side, it seemed a place out of an arctic Homer. The idea of thin ice was taken as seriously as was the belief in the Chinook traps.

Nevertheless, I saw after we'd been running hard for maybe as few as three or four minutes, what I refused to accept was bad ice ahead. Very quickly it became impossible for me to ignore or disbelieve. I shouted at the dogs and hauled on the brake but there was no stopping them. I tried to turn them but they were clearly going to run until they couldn't run anymore. I waved frantically to Antonia behind me and one runner cracked the ice. The sled tipped to one side and I fell off. Maybe I jumped, thinking it was all going. I can't honestly say. I suppose it was a little of both. I hit the ice and went through it like candy glass in a movie but the dogs and sled did not. Feeling my weight gone, the dogs slowed and stopped and turned to look at me. I have gone through the ice before—in shallower water—and everybody I know who runs dogs has gone through, too. If one remains calm, one flounders nine times out of ten like a walrus up onto firmer ice. I did so. I was so calm I was almost what you might call happy. The dogs had gathered in a circle: something was happening and they didn't like it. I could see Antonia grinning a grin of terrified determination in that clear cold blue sunlight. When she came to me I saw she was going to rush past and I lunged, knocking her off the sled and breaking two of her ribs. As we struggled back to shore, me a sodden thousand pounds and beginning to lose body heat, Antonia bent in pain, we hollered for the dogs to follow, but they were now afraid to move. I looked away and when I looked back they were going under. We watched as they scrabbled and pawed the ice, some of them getting up only to have it break or the weight of the other dogs yank them off. The sleds got hung up on chunks of ice, so it wasn't until spring that they sank. It's so deep there, two thousand feet deep, that I sometimes imagine them still sinking, the sleds now pulling them.

The day after the party I sharpened the teeth on one of Patrick's many chain saws, replaced its spark plug, and took down several trees. My mind was not on my work and I knew it ought to be, but I couldn't think of anything but the mistakes I had made, the foolish chances I'd taken, the poor judgment I'd exercised: the landing on a slope that was steeper than I expected, almost landing on the water with my wheels down, forgetting to tie the pontoons down and watching the plane drift away from shore—the list was endless. For a long time, it was Antonia's secret conviction that my biggest mistake had been knocking her from her sled. She never said explicitly whether with this remonstration she meant she could have steered the team to safety or that she would rather have gone down with them. Some nights I was sure she wished I had not been able to climb out—not that she wanted me dead, but that nobody should have survived such a tragedy.

Patrick came out after noon with another saw. He'd smoked some pot to overcome a hangover, and I flagged him down.

"You have to wear glasses and gloves," I said. He produced dramatically these safety items, flourishing the glasses from a shirt pocket and the gloves like a baseball player from a rear pants pocket. We saw Betty emerge from her house and slowly come toward us, bearing a tray on which we eventually made out a pitcher and glasses. The sky had been overcast but was clearing, and the sunlight sparkled on the crystal as the old woman made her way through the meadow. The sky was light blue, but deepening, almost before our eyes. I saw a car passing from one tunnel of trees to another and another far below us on the town road. I believed it was Antonia. I knew she would come back, if only to tell me she couldn't live without other people—a complaint I had heard many times before, and was ready to discount. Betty handed me a glass and winked at me. While we drank our lemonade, I gave Patrick a first course on timber cutting: how to make the cuts, how to hold the saw, where to stand, how to judge the way the tree would fall, how it might hop off its stump and fall another way entirely—then watched as he fired his saw up and leaned through some heavy brush around the base of a tree in a tight little stand with several others. He revved it a few times, then bore into the wood, the saw screaming, chips in a spray all around him. I looked up at the sky again. It was now a deep and clear blue. But such a blue, I said to myself, no longer troubles me. Patrick's saw changed its note, then fell to an idling pop and sputter. I watched him reposition himself. The car I thought was Antonia's appeared at the top of the drive but it was not Antonia. I looked up at the sky again and saw in that instant how I might atone for my sin. The crowns of the other trees in the stand were pushing against the crown of the tree in which Patrick was finishing the first cut. I saw that the force created by the other trees would cause the tree to fall in precisely the direction we had decided it would not—that it would fall toward Patrick. Trees fall much more quickly than you think they will, and I was quite sure I was about to save my brother-in-law's life. I began to walk toward him, waving my arms, not in alarm, because he hadn't begun the second crucial cut, but as if I were an assistant director saying, no, no, he wants to try it again, please.

The tree did not fall as we planned it to fall, and neither did it fall as I foresaw it would when I discovered my mistake. What it actually did was barber-chair. That was what old-timers used to call it. When Patrick's saw reached the middle of the trunk, the incredible force being exerted on it by the other trees caused it to split up the middle, straight up the trunk like a bolt of lightning in reverse. The freed half of the tree swung out like the footrest of a barber's chair, like a huge lever on a massive spring, a catapult's arm. It caught Patrick under his chin and hurled him though the air. He landed at my feet, all pulp and clay and blood and bits of white bone.

Patrick had wanted us to stay together, but why it should have mattered so much to him I can't say. He was angrier at his sister than I'd ever realized, angry for reasons I know I will never know—and he willed the molds to me. Antonia did not so much as want to look at the piece. I stupidly imagined for a while that we might weep over it and come together again. I pleaded with her, but she never came. I never saw her again. I made and sold three sets of bronze sled dogs, shipped one to Yellowknife, where they display it at the airport, and returned myself, on the proceeds, to the land over there far away—which I see clearly now is here.

the
free fall

I said, "I shall be wise," but it was far from me. That which is far off, and exceeding deep, Who can find it out?
—ECCLESIASTES 7:23-24

PART ONE: 1988
1

At first it was not hard to remember: the sudden rage—at once white-hot and infantile—at being caught in a knot of traffic in a blizzard at two in the morning, the dreamy release of superhuman speed through the bright, dry tunnel, the snow-slick curve on the other end, the sudden weightlessness as the tires lost the tiny ovals of their contact with the pavement, the instant of wild panic and then the retreat—orderly in its curious way, and swift—from sensation and emotional response—body tossed this way, then that way, then this way—as the car spun and slammed about like a carnival ride and seemed silently to disintegrate around him as it bore remorselessly down upon a semi—surely these things would stay with him. Surely he would never forget them. Especially that long, dark, electric fraction of a second in which he knew he had lost what was most dear to him, when, though his hands still gripped the wheel and worked it with pathetic violence, the matter lapsed irretrievably from his purview and he knew he had lost control. The trajectories of automobile and self could no longer be plotted; their destinations were a mystery. He was no longer a citizen in a motor vehicle of which he was sole owner and proprietor, doing what he pleased—hurtling through time and space with so much reckless hubris as to make it seem the clock were going backward and he drawing near a moment and place where something had once begun and would again begin—but rather a felon, under arrest, detouring to a hospital for a moment of medical sport with a nurse whose white smock was stained with coffee, who smelled strongly of coffee, and who dressed wounds the existence of which upon his person he had not suspected. Then, while preparing to take a sample of his blood, she sipped from a chipped white cup that appeared never to have been cleaned, not in a decade at least, and gestured at an even filthier coffeemaker, in which perhaps a century of bitter sediment had accumulated, urging the cop to help himself.

But he did: he did forget nearly all of it.

Taking a last sip, the nurse patted up a vein in his fore-arm and inserted the needle. Gary Leen looked carefully out the corner of his eye at the dangling apparatus: nor-mally, needles put him away. Even the thought of giving blood could make him nauseous, soak him in cold sweat. "It's always the tough guys," a doctor once kidded him, after reviving him with smelling salts. Leen assured him that he was not a tough guy. Whatever it was that he was—there were a number of compelling and attractive ideas, chief among them in those days *altruistic public servant, maver-ick apparatchik, loose-cannon liberal*—he was not a tough guy. And yet for a moment—a sense of minutes slowly ticking past but which could only have been a blink of an eye—it seemed as if by an act of miraculous, saintly iron will that he could withhold the blood a displeased authority de-manded of him, as if he had been stabbed in the heart but was not bleeding, something out of a saga, a hero.

As he watched the cop's eyes twinkle over his cup of coffee and the nurse do a double take, he thought he might actually join them in their subdued mirth. Were they not after all a brother cop and a sister nurse? And were they not simply seeing to the order of things, to a social con-tinuity and decency that were indescribably dear to him? What if everybody acted the way he had? Leen wanted to laugh good-naturedly, admit his great foolishness, his ridiculously impaired judgment—the stupidity of it, the deadly seriousness of it, the crime of it!—but in the end roar with laughter and confess his secret plan, announce his candidacy for some obscure but important state office that would eventually catapult him into Congress. Were the wheels not moving? Had they not been moving for some time, and in the direction of public, elective office? Was he not picking up speed? All those things were true. He thought he might chuckle and say, You know everything now! When my opponent for county comptroller suggests I am a no-good drunken bum, we three can remember what I was really like, how candid and reasonable, how warmly human and sincerely repentant I was, here in this ugly, coffee-stinking room in the middle of a stormy winter's night. Vote for me!

Leen looked at them fondly, wryly, as if indeed minutes and not seconds had passed and they were in on the monologue . . . but they had become, in those few almost hallucinatorily lurid moments, characters in a fairy tale, perhaps Hansel and Gretel, he didn't know, and he closed his bloodshot eyes. They were out to stuff him into an oven, that much was clear.

He flinched and shuddered and blood filled the syringe. Real time resumed.

"Organs shrink with fear!" bellowed the nurse in the deepest voice he had ever heard come from a woman, filling her coffee cup. "Blood literally freezes in the veins in shock and terror!"

"Survival instinct," said the cop, eyes twinkling merrily over his cup. "It's like flight or fight but you can't do either one so you lock up like a fist." He set his cup down and made one to help Leen understand, but it seemed vaguely threatening. "Like you're hanging on to something, Gary, for your life."

And as if at last room had been made for it in the poisoned hydraulics of his body, guilt and remorse flooded over him. It was all he could do, tough guy that he was

or was not, not to sob. He was out of order. He was inde-
cent. He was frightened. But with what he imagined was
brisk, indifferent professionalism, he queried the cop re
the time frame regarding the current suspension of liberty. His head wavered slightly with the effort, and the
cop looked at him sideways—not unkindly, but as if Leen
had interrupted him. He acted as if he hadn't understood
the question.

"How long," Leen asked, *"before the point at which I am to be
remanded to my own custody. I've got a campaign to run."*

That was the strangest part of the evening: the sarcastic disdain, the loose-jointed but wooden-gestured
performance of a little sitcom of contempt—or was it actual contempt?—that he feigned for the man who had ap-
prehended him, the woman who was gathering evidence
against him, the entities who would soon begin to punish
him, the laws and order of the state whose famed waters
flowed, he believed, in his very veins.

2

Leen was married to a woman named Leah Le Blanc, who
was descended from Hollywood psychiatrists, and who
had come to Minnesota, where a branch of the family
traded in leather goods, because she did not want to be
a Hollywood psychiatrist. An inherited but equally fer-
vent admiration for Hubert H. Humphrey (he had been
her mother's dinner guest several times and raised a great
deal of money while seeming completely at ease with the

comedians from another generation who made up her practice, an ease that Leah found almost supernatural, fearing them as she did) and a twofold concern, inspired by a biology teacher who would one day have a movie filmed of his life, about the extinction of staple seed stocks and corporate ownership of genetically altered replacements, made Minnesota a good choice for someone disgusted with movies and wishing to feel exiled. Double-majoring at the U of M in history (thesis on Yiddish theater) and political science (origins of the New Deal, focusing on Floyd B. Olson, Minnesota's governor during the worst of the Depression, who declared a moratorium on farm fore-closures eighteen days after Leen's paternal grandfather lost his), she graduated with honors, studied economics for a while, then jumped to the law school. They met at a bulletin board outside one of the big West Bank lecture halls. She was looking for a rust-eaten pickup and wished at the same time to unload the Mercedes-Benz she'd gotten as a graduation present. Leen owned such a truck (a three-quarter-ton Chevy) and desperately wanted, at that time in his life—he'd gotten his GED only a few years earlier and was inhaling night courses, "culture," and the trap-pings of "good taste" at a pace that might have been comic had his emotional engine not been screaming way past its redline—a classy car. The bumper stickers on Leah's golden convertible indicated political sentiments closely allied with his—notably the recent power line protests, which had farmers running surveyors off their land with shotguns and off the road with pickup trucks—and they began to see each other.

Eight years later, Leah, embarrassed and weary, patted her husband's head uncertainly as he sobbed on his
knees before her, begging forgiveness. "I can't help but
notice," she said after a while, in a kindly tone of voice,
"that the only time you shut up is when you're crying your
eyes out."

Leen started to say something but she cut him off
with an imperious, exasperasted gesture: "No, *please do*
shut up."

It was true. His mother had told him when he was very
young that he was a very *very* sensitive and very very *intelligent* boy, and he'd believed it, experiencing these somehow contradictory if not altogether hostile qualities as
idealism and perfectionism and becoming consequently,
with the help of a natural expressiveness in the play of
his features, something of an after-dinner speaker. How
could she have been so wrong? Had she been rendered entirely senseless by maternal love? And his father, who told
him over and over again how blessed he was, a young man
who could muck out the barn *and* think independently:
Had he chosen to ignore the weakness of character and
the loose screws because he loved his son? How could he
have failed to notice that he was a sociopath? Leen felt
now that he would never make a speech or take a drink
again, that he would remain penitent, humble, and quiet
for the rest of his life, would come to understandings
with himself and improve himself and be as he should
have been all along, the sensible and diligent boy right out
of Thornton Wilder, raised with love and patience, tread-
ing meekly but surely on solid ground, a decent man and
a good citizen.

A memory, unlooked for, overtook him: cold wooden pews, gray light filtering through stained glass, the number of the hymns to be sung on big oaken Ten Commandments-style tablets hung on the wall behind the pulpit with its shiny microphone, the huge painting of the Christ with his golden hair shampooed and conditioned, his lips too red, floating through the air, the moaning, rustling close of a hymn, coughing, a dropped hymnal, a pastor in a weak but miked voice, elevated in the way of a bad, or at least an uncertain, an apprehensive actor, offering an anecdote on the insufficiency of works alone with regard to eternal salvation. "We must have faith," the pastor said quietly into the mike, which crackled its message out over the silent immobile congregation. And Leen looked up to see that his wife had lost hers. She seemed to look down at him from some unimaginable height, her angrily laughing face peering over a precipitous judge's bench. Clearly she had once had faith. Clearly she had loved him. As his parents had. How did one go about removing oneself from such embraces, with such consistency and speed? Perhaps it was because he had no faith. It was possible he'd never had any. But he was stubborn, he was determined to act himself out of the black muttering gutter, back into the bright garments and sunshine of health and wealth and wisdom. And he would, in fact, in a matter of eight more years, have a campaign to run.

3

Leen took his daughter, Lucy, to the yard where the wrecked car had been impounded. She seemed very bored, but asked penetrating questions about insurance. He looked at her and smiled sadly. She was eight and often surprised him with her knowledge of practical adult matters—matters that secretly troubled her father to the point where he would have to ignore them—and intellectual concerns. When she'd been in the first grade, she'd asked him about "Bleeding Kansas," and he'd walked her through it, amazed and asking questions like "Do you know what the Civil War was about?" taking effects farther and farther back, getting progressively more complicated, she nodding and saying yes to every important point until it seemed she understood Bleeding Kansas, the puritan capitalism of the industrial North, the arrogant aristocracy of the agrarian South, a country full of people eager, after two hundred years of fantastic tolerance, for violence. They'd been watching a baseball game ("Why is Kansas City in Missouri and not Kansas?"). A pitcher had been pulled and conducted a tantrum in the dugout. "Look at the little baby," Leen had jeered. There was no place in the National Pastime for such immaturity. Lucy responded, "He's not a little baby, he's a good pitcher." Leen snorted that he was in fact a big baby, skilled as a pitcher or not. "No," she said, "you're the big baby."

He walked around the car, wondering how he could have stepped from such destruction as unscathed as he had, came back to his daughter, zipped up her parka. He wanted to explain what was going to happen in a gentle way, but Lucy, he suspected, was way ahead of him, and would see the gentleness as pathetically false. So he told her simply that they had liability insurance and no more, and let her fill in the blanks.

She seemed briskly indifferent to the news.

4

Leah was in the nation's captial during the Thanksgiving holiday that year, deposing people in the secretary of agriculture's office—here one can see clearly a difference in trajectories that might affect a marriage—so Leen and his daughter went to a revolving restaurant atop a hotel in downtown Saint Paul. Half of their table's orbit offered a view of the Mississippi, brilliant blue and smoking faintly in a field of blinding white. Leen hadn't had a drink for two weeks and was blissfully happy; the vision of the cold river in the pristine landscape struck him as a perfect metaphor for his new life.

The broad ring on which the tables were arranged was like a stately Disney amusement: very slowly they approached Dessert Land, Omelette Land, Ham and Turkey Land, Service Land with its mountains of silverware and trays of ice water. They ate hungrily, and after they'd eaten, Leen dabbed at his face with the heavy linen napkin. "Sprayed food all over the place!" he laughed. "Anything caught in my mustache?" He wondered for a moment if he should shave the mustache, that it suggested something about his character he no longer wished to advertise. Then he grew philosophical—a habit which, he was only just beginning to understand, was not altogether benign and which was certainly part of a web of habits that began with the urge to cut up, to amuse and influence, passed through various types of self-aggrandizement, and ended in self-absorption, rage, and paranoia. The big, clean windows came around again. "That area down there?" he pointed with a thumb over his shoulder, "is where the poor workers lived."

"Poor workers," said Lucy. "Poor, poor workers."

Because he was who he was, and because he had worked for unions, grassroots political organizing teams, and now a political party, it was possible she'd heard this before. And though she'd been conceived the night her parents were released from a jail in which they'd rested for a night and a day for an act of civil disobedience, it was also possible that she was a child of what would later be called "the go-go years." Leen therefore regarded her with real concern and doubt. She seemed cheerful with the surfeit of food in her belly, full of *gemütlichkeit*. Wondering if she would someday become obese, he went on.

"The river flooded them out all the time, because they were sinful, I guess. Up on that bluff there on the other side of the river?" He gestured with his thumb again, then turned in his seat and searched the white distance. "There is a very fine steakhouse there indeed. Have to take you there sometime." The thought of eating a steak there and not having a martini clouded his face for a moment. He saw himself drunk and incoherent, demanding another drink while his elephantine daughter stuffed her face. "Remind me and we'll go. I don't know, there's something about rivers, don't you think? Floating rather than falling? Make you wonder about time? The famous River of Time?"

Lucy looked out the window for a moment, then back at her father, waiting.

Leen was an autodidact, took an autodidact's pleasure in referring to himself as an autodidact, and in lecturing casually about the things he'd learned—something like an after-dinner speaker before dinner. So he continued. "Where did it all begin? Where will it all end? A man falls down. We ask why. Answer: he fell down because he was drunk! Why would being drunk, though, hang on, make him fall down? Most people are content to stop with the idea that alcohol affects one's sense of balance. But there are other questions to ask. Is falling on one's face necessarily the worst thing that can happen to a person? Why was the man drunk in the first place? Because he was weak? What made him feel weak? Unhappiness? What made him feel unhappy? Had he lost his job? Was he simply shy and lonely? Had his dog been—" he stopped himself. "Maybe he didn't have a happy childhoo—" He stopped himself again. Lucy supplied the missing "d." He ignored her. "You ask yourself why to all these questions, going back, back, waaaaaay back!" he laughed, "and you get to the question of the origin of the universe, and what have you learned, honey? That the question was flawed somehow? That it led only to confusion? That it, well, you see what I'm saying, don't you?"

They passed through Dessert Land, which had been pillaged. What was left looked fake, waxen, inedible. The big windows came around. Even if the river only looked clean, that was enough. It flowed an unimaginable distance. Where it ended, things were very different. It might be, for instance, hot.

5

Leen's punishments were perfunctory but severe. He took a bus to the courthouse and rose when the state of Minnesota declared itself against him. *Everybody?* he thought. The assistant DA surprised his lawyer by bringing the driver of the semi off which he'd bounced into the room. The truck driver said he thought Leen had encouraged them all to leave the scene of the crime. Leen's lawyer asked him if this was true and Leen said no, of course not, my car was in pieces, I clearly wasn't going anywhere, what a ridiculous idea. Then the young and zealous prosecutor brought the cop in, who said Leen was so drunk and scared he'd pissed in his pants. To this Leen replied that he'd had a cup of coffee between his legs and while crashing had been unable or unwilling to keep it from spilling. Because "spilling" and "unwilling" rhymed, it almost sounded as if he were being facetious, so he explained to everybody that his car didn't have cup holders due to its great age, and that he was therefore in the habit of holding his coffee between his legs. His nerves were beginning to fray and snap, and he suppressed a giggle by making a rather exaggerated frown. He appeared to have an answer for everything but could not defend himself against the fundamental wrongdoing, and so was found guilty: he had to spend another forty-eight hours in jail, had his license revoked, was ordered to perform twenty-five hours of public service, to attend a series of classes on driving and alcoholism, and go to four meetings of Alcoholics Anonymous. When the judge asked him if he understood his crime and its punishment, he could not speak. This sudden inability surprised him, and he froze. Only his eyes moved, back and forth in panic between judge and lawyer. The judge suggested that perhaps Leen's lawyer could explain things to him one more time, and Leen smiled his agreement, nodding happily and eagerly, as if he could not speak English but had made a dramatic, complicated, crucially important wish known with gestures.

The public service he performed—because he'd had experience writing press releases for various political and nonprofit organizations—was to write a brochure about the public service components of new sentencing guidelines. In the class he learned that nearly every American with a driver's license had more than likely driven a vehicle while if not legally drunk then seriously impaired with drink, and that treatment of alcoholics in the United States was based largely on research conducted by one man, who had hypothesized sixty-five basic types of alcoholic, then run out of funding after defining only five, leaving the remaining sixty unexplored and possibly misunderstood by the society seeking to help them.

To satisfy the AA requirement, he'd been given little yellow cards that called for the date and location of the meeting, and the signature of another alcoholic. But because he'd already characterized himself as just the one in a thousand who'd gotten caught, and certainly as an example of one of the unidentified and misunderstood basic types—possibly therefore not even "an alcoholic" at all!—he skipped the meetings and forged the signatures. Strangely, he went to the trouble of copying real signatures—a couple from the Declaration of Independence, a couple from direct mail advertising letters, holding originals and cards up against a sunlit window—and a fictional one using his right hand (Leen was remarkably ambidextrous), prompting his wife to ask him why.

He told her that the "anonymous" part was to be taken seriously, and that the state had no right to force him in effect to force them, the anonymous alcoholics, to identify themselves. Technically, a first name was as far as a guy could be compelled to go. Leen saw he was in danger of being unmeek in this argument and tried to backpedal, spewing nonsense about the sixty-five basic types and mewling about the real, the actual nature of a crime that was committed on a regular basis by lots and lots of people. He included the phrase *from all walks of life*, and that was, he saw then but only understood later, the last straw for her. They remained married for several more years, divorcing only after the riots in International Falls that are the climactic event and nominal subject of this adventure, but when Leah saw that her husband was just going to keep talking that day, when she suspected the humble contrition was little more than an act he'd committed himself to, like a Method actor (that is to say, with overwhelming psychological resources and emotional commitment to the point of delusion, but only to a character at a crucial but almost indistinguishable remove from the self), she found her respect for her husband weakening dramatically. And there is nothing more fleeting than love, of course, so that was gone too.

PART TWO: 1980
6

Leah Le Blanc was not a level-headed, practical, good-natured woman, but she appeared to be, and won friends

and influenced people as if she were. She was also exceptionally good-looking, which is a condition that encour-
ages people to play along with one.

The marriage was understood by friends (and, eventually, onlookers) in this way: Leen offered Leah a lot in
the way of authenticity in places and situations where a
child of Hollywood psychiatrists might stand out—perhaps suspiciously, certainly ostentatiously. And without
any doubt or qualification or reservation, it was said that
Leah promoted the growth of something in Leen, and accelerated it, that would otherwise have lain dormant. Had
she not met him, he would never have been anything but
a frustrated and unhappy after-dinner speaker. Her sanction of his mind, and the little dramas in which he spoke
it—her approval, admiration, affection—allowed him to
think well of himself.

Early in the romance, early in the spring of 1980, they
drove west from the Twin Cities to a little bank on the
prairie, in a windbreak of a town and very much an island,
that day, in a sea of white, called Montevideo. Three coun-
ties—Lac Qui Parle, Yellow Medicine, and Chippewa—met
just south of the town, but there were no mountains, and
the reference to the capital of Uruguay was lost on everybody. The day had started out with a kind of warmth in
the air and a softness in the sky, but the wind had shifted
violently so that by noon it was an icy gale straight from
Alberta—a clipper, these winds were called—and it picked
up the snow from drifts like foam on waves. A protest
was being staged at the bank, a sit-in. The theme was the
demise of the family farm, and the event was a foreclo-
sure. There were more than a hundred and possibly as

many as two hundred people there—during the speeches, when the bank was closing, and the state troopers and *posse comitatus* representatives of the Minnesota Militia had arrived—maybe thirty farmers and as many wives and sons and daughters, several van- and carloads of protesters from various colleges and community organizations (Leah and Leen represented UMPIRG, the Upper Midwest Public Intererst Research Group, and the Seed Saver Exchange), representatives from the American Agriculture Movement and COACT (Citizen Organizations Acting Together), and, surprisingly, some people of influence from the Democratic-Farmer-Labor Party, most of whom the couple recognized from neighborhood and district caucuses, along with a few known only by reputation and sightings at state conventions. There were two newspaper reporters as well, and, just as the bank was closing, a TV news crew from Mankato, whose lights, as the early winter night fell, increased the general sense that some kind of emergency operation was under way, that some minor disaster had happened, or was about to. The people from the vans mainly stayed outside, patrolling the sidewalks, drinking coffee from dented and scratched aluminum urns in the back of the vans, but there was a good deal of movement in and out of the bank, making the foyer cold enough for the snow brought in clinging to gigantic boots to melt very slowly. Almost everybody wore several layers of clothing, turtlenecks and flannel shirts and ski sweaters, the outermost garment usually a down-filled parka—some bright with the insane colors of sporting gear, others dark with soil and the grease of toil, tufts of dirty white synthetic fill exposed in ripped seams and torn pockets. Many people wore stocking caps as well, and some of the picketers wore full-face balaclava-style ski masks, giving the impression with their loud and sudden entries of a daring daylight robbery that was somehow not going off as planned, due to unaccountable delay, a held-up holdup.

The pale cold sunlight that filled the bank's lobby became harsher and harsher as the angle of its descent changed and struck the glass doors and illuminated not some bright biblical scene but the streaks of cleaning fluid, grease from a thousand hands, frozen grime, remnants of translucent tape where flyers had once been displayed, and the somehow terrible, somehow ominous, reversed lettering of the bank's name. On a sunny spring morning it would seem a joyous transparency, a purposeful clarity, but in that quickly cooling and weakening light, it was merely confusing and unsettling, striking Leah and Leen as a warning in an incomprehensible, Cyrillic-like alphabet, as if they were not in Minnesota but in the Soviet Union, soon to be arrested and deported to Siberia. They looked at the doors opening and closing, opening and closing, angry people milling with cheerful people, the nervous and uncertain with the curious and excited, emotions swirling chaotically, shifting back and forth from face to face, as if being transferred by some unknown power for unknown reasons, rippling with an almost mechanical quality through groups of blank faces in some kind of hand-cranked magic lantern animation of an Ensor painting, lighting up here a head, hung low and shaking stubbornly or raised up in hysteria or exaltation, or there a hand at the end of an arm flung out in a statuesque, Lenin-like gesture, or part of some intricate and impenetrable act of mimesis or maddeningly inscrutable charade, the tellers congregated at a desk in a far corner in the attitudes of a coffee break that would go on until further notice, a kind of coffee break on bivouac, all the miniature doors of their windows closed as if they were making-believe in a little playhouse of a bank and that these doors somehow made all the difference. "This is a holdup!" "We're closed!"

It was all a little too much for Leen: that kind of crowd in those early days when he needed a steady intake of liquor to find crowds of any sort less than unnerving, civil disobedience when his reticent Lutheran bones ached with the urge to obey the prince and his earthly commandments, emotion mixing in unpredictable and volatile ways with principle—and Leah, with whom he was only just becoming comfortable, was talking loudly, almost brazenly or haughtily, with the DFLers in a way Leen already knew could not easily include him, so he made his way through the lobby and out the doors.

The clipper caught the big unwieldy signs of the picketers and made them bang and pop and swing about like weather vanes. Above the bank the flags of Minnesota and the United States of America snapped as loudly as if there were firecrackers concealed in them, and glowed with the light of the setting sun. There weren't many pedestrians, but car traffic was moving very slowly if at all through the intersection, drivers and passengers looking but pretending not to look with that stiff-necked and wide-eyed posture in which they seemed to be both ready to cause, and fearfully bracing for, mishap. Occasionally a horn would call ambiguously, ragged and forlorn and remote as anything in Wagner, and the picketers would respond like a stewing and confused choir, voices instantly lost in the wind.

The feeling that he had escaped something was a familiar and soothing one, but as Leen walked and the sounds of the intersection diminished rapidly, the notes becoming clearer and clearer and softer and softer as the air seemed to grow colder and colder, he was surprised by how greatly it troubled him. It had always lain perilously close to a feeling of fear and panicked flight, but that day it was in sharp contrast as well to the feeling that Leah had not only not escaped, not fled, but entered the bank as if the chances for progress, for some kind of clear and gratifying action, or even simple selfish aggrandizement, had never been greater, as if that room on that day at that hour was the only place in all the world she wanted to be.

She entered restaurants and living rooms in the same way. She rejected tables they'd been shown to, dismissed items from menus as they were described to her, and took issue with every check. He begged waiters not to trouble themselves, accepted cold hamburgers, and tipped lavishly in the hope that people whom he would never again meet would like him anyway. She spoke uninhibitedly of intimate matters even when the tables were quite close and the atmosphere hushed with prim Nordic sophistication, and took clear and shameless pleasure in eavesdropping, while he nervously gulped his drinks. Part of this was just standard-issue Borscht Belt takes on a big-city Jew coming to the Little House on the Prairie, but while she could do that routine, and appear to enjoy it despite the fear of comedians that had dominated her childhood, what really animated her in a room was a nearly sexual love of the democratic political process and nearly religious embrace of progressive policies and liberal ideals.

Leen walked several blocks into a neighborhood of small homes, cottages built in the late forties and early fifties, remarkably tiny, well kept and mostly tidy, curtains in every window, and warm lights, smoke puffing from chimneys palely against the darker smoke of the twilit sky. He could see farmland at the end of the street, two or three blocks off, and walked toward it. He crossed the street and could now see flat white land spreading out to the south and west, so suddenly that it seemed to be expanding, surging in some kind of silent tidal flow to the horizon, a slowly seething red band and a faint pencil line smudged here and there with the trees of farmhouse windbreaks. An old wooden slat fence sagged against the red-painted iron rods of a barbed-wire fence marking off a small feedlot. He could see no cattle, but smelled them, and found the smell comforting as a drink. He felt them near, almost as if they'd been standing there at the fence just before he appeared at the other end of the street, and might reappear if only he waited patiently and quietly. The shouts and the honking horns had died away so completely that all he could hear was the wind moving the snow. Then he could hear something clanking in the nearest building, a feed bin banging closed, but it wasn't enough, he wanted more, he wanted to hear them breathing, and swishing their tails and lowing and tapping their hooves on the concrete floor. The longer he waited, the happier he felt. Both of Leen's parents had been raised on farms. He came from a long line of farmers and whatever else, he thought, might be true about him, in his heart he felt he was one of them. The best bed was straw, the best blanket, animal heat, the best conversation, silence.

At least he imagined it to be so. He also knew he was a farm boy with what would commonly be described, and genuinely understood, around the hearths of the folk he'd grown up with, as a real Hollywood Jew for a girfriend. He felt on the verge of great sophisticated politicking, but the truth was that the family farm was dead, long dead, and that his wish to spend time with livestock was in fact a yearning to die, disguised as an idea of living simply and quietly in a world he knew did not—could not possibly—exist anymore. It was a fairy tale, but what is most remarkable in this episode of his and Leah's life is at once a vulnerability to fairy tales and an overwhelming desire to make them come true.

7

He walked quickly back toward the bank, and as he did, he could hear the shouting swell again and again over the roar of the wind and the unintelligible exhortations of somebody with a bullhorn. He was no longer uneasy. He was excited and happy, and this is the fatal crux, the moment of transformation—there can be no other word for what happened even if he appeared only to have cheered up or relaxed or gotten a second wind. He felt suddenly and clearly that he belonged, that he was needed, that he was capable and resourceful and principled. He bore no one enmity: not the town cops, the sheriff and his deputies, and the state troopers, not the bankers, the loan officers and tellers, the real estate agents, the developers, the bureaucrats, the lawyers, the doctors, the nurses, the auctioneers and the implement dealers, the seed and feed men, the teachers, the car dealers and mechanics, not the mayor and the members of the town council, not the mean drunks and indifferent bartenders in the bars nor the kindly pastors in the churches, not the luminous, imperious television crew, not the beauticians and barbers and butchers and bakers, the short-order cooks and the waitresses and the snowplow drivers and the utility maintenance crews. The slaughterhouse and the library seemed one thing to him and that one thing was brilliant and amazing. The constant struggle of negotiation and compromise, understanding and misunderstanding, the rise and fall of sympathy and anger, the tide of thought and blood and right and wrong and greed and mercy—he was stunned by the complexity and vastness of it as surely as if someone had struck him a staggering blow. Which of course someone did, but not until later, when he was able to receive it as a natural extension of forces beyond his control, as a physical manifestation of the great power of fear and panic, deflect and absorb it and feel no pain.

(The pain would be felt by others: less than a year later, in a town just a few miles southwest of Montevideo, two bankers would be ambushed and murdered by a man and his son, incompetent farmers to be sure, but just as surely part of "the order" he worshipped.)

Leah, laughing so fiercely he was quite sure something was wrong, grabbed him by the arm and pulled him violently through a knot of shouting people, then pushed him directly into the space of a three-way argument between the sheriff, who looked like a hard-drinking but no-nonsense Swede-and-Chippewa crossblood, an older man in a suit, wearing a clipped gray mustache and adopting a military bearing, whom Leen took to be a senior banker, and another man, also older but wearing overalls, the charismatic farmer who had organized the protest and who would, ten years later, become one of Minnesota's senators. All three men were talking fiercely and at once. Strangely, Leen could hear plainly and clearly everything they said, above the din, as if he had United Nations-style headphones on, or was following along with a transcript. At some point he began to speak, gesturing and intoning like an actor, coming up with bits and pieces of things he'd read, from Schumacher's Buddhist economics to Erikson on Gandhi and Luther, Frederick Turner, some half-baked notions about the regenerative qualities of violence—even Vicki Hearne, shouting over and over again that *were* no bad dogs because there *could be* no bad dogs. That was when the *posse comitatus* lunkhead either fell against him or shoved him, and he stepped backward into a table with such speed and grace that he was on top of it before he knew it, making a speech that began with an adaptation of Shylock's cry to the court—"A farmer is a human being, isn't he? Stick a pitchfork up a farmer's ass and he'll stick one up yours!"—and went on to briefly outline the world of primitive, intensive manual labor in which a thousand people labored night and day to feed a thousand people, and a glimmering technocracy in which one person labored hardly at all to feed the same thousand, who, because they had nothing to do, were dependent on oppressive welfare. He described a sci-fi dystopia in which one subhuman *farmer* worked a console of three buttons: the first fed the cattle and hogs and chickens on a farm so big it took up all of North Dakota, the second sucked all the shit from their box cages, and the third slaughtered them. He asked the people in the bank if that was the kind of food they wanted to eat. He assured them that he didn't want to eat that kind of food! That was like eating hate and fear! Where was the protein in that? Where were the vitamins and minerals in hate and fear?

Leen actually said that. There is a clean and clear videotape of the speech. The spin he put on "farmer" was worthy of—and probably inspired by—John Belushi, who was alive and well on *Saturday Night Live* then. Following the speech, he was wrestled off the table by deputies. A score of protesters were arrested—good guys and bad guys alike. The farmer who would one day become a senator took Leen aside at one feverish point and said, "This is a great thing you're doing. Don't ever give up. I won't if you won't." And that was the beginning.

8

Two nights later, Lucy, as mentioned earlier, was conceived. Leah graduated from law school, passed her bar exams, and took the job with FLAG (Farmers' Legal Aid Group). She and Leen were married on an island in Lake Superior, at the cabin of a friend of theirs who had married into a family of department store heirs. A cousin lived on the next property over—he too would become, before the end of the millennium, a United States senator. This is of course when Leen began to think of running for office himself. It was only natural. Because another friend was the son of a man who sat on the board of the Hormel meat company, he found himself acting as a liaison between that board and several ad hoc committees formed in the upheaval of the meatpackers' strike, a strike that was violent and bitter and protracted enough to warrant a feature-length documentary that was distributed internationally and won a prize at Cannes, and in which both Leah and he are briefly interviewed. Leah did some work that favorably impressed one of the partners in a firm founded by one of the state's most successful fund-raisers, got herself an interview with that man and an invitation to dinner. She was offered a job with the firm and declined on the grounds that she was in the middle of something she was committed to seeing through. The fund-raiser called Leah's mother, but she wouldn't budge. Leen worked for a while in the state capitol building, running the news bureau, and met a woman who eventually made him a regular guest on a weekly public television show devoted to local politics. He was well known for his speech at the bank, and found it increasingly easy to be entertaining and in some instances even charming while speaking his mind. The energy begat energy, and the more confident he felt the more boldly he spoke. In the hothouse of the TV show, he found he could instantly figure out who was in the room with him, what they would say, how far they would go, wait for them to draw the line, then dance across it. If someone was learned, he was more learned; if someone was frank, he was reckless; if someone dared to think of himself as a risk-taker, he was crazy. After living in a tent on the outskirts of Rochester for a week with the future senator—they couldn't afford the hotels the rest of the state conventioneers were in—he was asked to manage his first campaign—for state representative, which they lost—and quickly followed his man into Jesse Jackson's Rainbow Coalition, co-chairing the Minnesota effort. He and Leah spent some time partying with one of the Minnesota Vikings, a junkyard dog linebacker who was secretly a well-read liberal with political ambitions, and his coterie, one of whom was the daughter of yet another senator (retired) and presidential candidate. Leen had several affairs, culminating with that daughter, and had to drink himself down every night, had to drink himself to sleep, had to drink to keep the motor running and the lights on for a quick start the next day. He was at once ascending and descending, and when he smashed his car up and was arrested for driving while intoxicated, he thought privately that he was not at all "out of control" but merely "going too fast." Which is not to say that his contrition was not genuine. It was. Once the first few months of blissful sobriety passed, he lost forty-five pounds because he couldn't bring himself to eat. At the same time, the contrition was political. That it was political did not make it less genuine. All behavior was an act of one kind or another, and all action in a society is political. Another eight years passed, in which he refrained from drink, grew increasingly influential within the party and hopelessly addicted to the improvised performance of spectacles of audacious and truculent will where no true valor could be counted on, daredevilry where there was no real faith, and the belief that he could, if he moved swiftly and adroitly enough, maintain the order of things around him—and, by secret mad midnight extensions, the world—on his own markedly deteriorating terms. Quite sure no harm would come of it, he began to drink again.

PART THREE: 1996
9

Leen sat in the soft and cool-colored light of a windowless conference room, listening to presentation after muted presentation, swiveling ever so faintly in his padded chair by flexing his toes. This was a very large and important meeting—representatives from a dozen unions, as many state legislators from the DFL caucus, staffers, and a handful of agency directors, someone from the Legislative Coordinating Committee, and Leen, who had just been asked to run a campaign for the United States Senate. Because the candidate was the darkest of horses, no one was surprised that he had chosen an equally untried campaign manager, so while no one was out to positively hurt his feelings, Leen was being largely ignored. They were in a very small but magnificent old room. The minute movements of certain muscles in his toes and consequently the chair were all Leen could manage. It was standing room only, and no one used the microphone that had been provided. Next to him sat the woman from the LCC, a trooper from one of several squadrons of willing women who had seemed for the last two or three years to be coming up out of the trenches at him, with whom he'd slept, for whom he'd secured the position, and who never missed an opportunity to display a disgusted loathing for him that could not possibly have been as theatrical at its source and in rehearsal as it was in public performance. The purpose of the meeting was to prepare for a high-profile convention, during which bleeding-heart progressives would come out swinging like the Teamsters they claimed to represent. Union membership was in steep decline in those years, and the first question they'd addressed was why: why, why, why, which effect are we talking about and which cause do we nail. Once that was answered, they would move on to such issues as when things might bottom out, and what might be done when they did. Panel and seminar topics included deregulation, affirmative action, welfare reform and the organization of these new kinds of workers, the nature of "service" work and "information" work, a new working definition of a "minimum wage," the billion-dollar drug-testing industry, the historical exclusion of minorities and women by union policy makers, the steady shifting of the tax burden onto the poorest third of the workers and the parallel accumulation of wealth amongst the richest one percent—and how, finally, not to appear pathetic to the go-getters of the go-go years.

Leen thought everybody in the room looked like a go-getter. It made him uneasy to think so, and therefore sarcastic in his participation, his sense of solidarity and belief in the system in real jeopardy, but that was who was in the room: management. His ambitions were no secret, and he had demonstrated on more than one occasion what a grandstander he could be if it suited his needs at a particular moment, but he could not help but feel the fear and the treachery in the air: they were not trying to find ways to save the unions—they were trying to find ways to save themselves. He felt it in the pit of his stomach, a nauseating, guilt-ridden anxiety, betrayal and abandonment as heartbreaking as anything he'd done to Leah—and yet this was the game into which he had absolutely to be dealt. He needed apparatus and consensus—without them he was a clown by day, a philandering drunk at night. He needed something else, but was not sure what that might be. The candidate in his moneyless-ness, in his familiarity with and dependence on rank-and-file workers and the actual blades of dandelion-emaciated grass that made up the vaunted grassroots movements of legend and fable, seemed to promise fulfillment of this inchoate need—to suggest at least that he knew where a man could find a strap to hold the beam and yoke of his plow together.

His talk had been on the romance of union-busting. "I'm going up north," he'd said, looking at his watch, "in just a couple of hours, to a place where a strike, believe it or not, is actually taking place. An international contractor based in Alabama, BE&K, has been hired by Boise Cascade to build a new papermaking facility up there in Frostbite Falls. $535 million. BE&K is famous for what, can anyone tell me?" He grinned around the room. "Union-busting. That's right." He was trying hard not to make a speech. "They give seminars on it, as a free service. Talk about long-term thinking! They're bringing in out-of-state nonunion people, and most of the locals, who are generations deep in their unions, are at the boiling point. It's a wildcat strike so of course they hate us now too. By us I mean of course not just their union's leadership but the whole system of so-called fair play associated with it, the whole show. Law and order. Law and order is for people who haven't had their eyes opened. It's a real laboratory for a study of the uses and abuses of violence."

His former friend spoke up.

"*Uses?*"

"Figure of speech."

"I should hope so!"

"Laboratory for study of the abuse of—"

"Violence can't be anything *other than abuse*—"

"Good point."

"I mean it's redundant, isn't it?"

"Good, yes, point. I—"

"And it's what, a laboratory up there? Is that what you said? '*A laboratory*'?"

"OH CAN WE PLEASE BE REALISTIC FOR ONCE? YOU SHOVE SOMEONE, NINETY-NINE TIMES OUT OF A HUNDRED THEY WILL SHOVE BACK!"

The common perception of those go-getters willing to think about the strike at all was that the wildcatters were behaving like dinosaurs, and one of them ventured to say so, in a silence made uneasy (Leen thought) by the transfer of his own to the room. Another man said he thought "dinosaur" was going a bit far. Leen said that the dinosaurs were all going to vote Republican for the next fifty years if they weren't careful—but it was too late, he felt himself falling and gripped the sides of the chair, grinning remorselessly now, effect to cause to effect to cause, taking it all the way back to the origins of the universe.

10

Driving north, he felt a lightening of limbs and outlook both, a loosening from the top of the neck down across the shoulders and out to the fingertips, down his spine and through his groin and thighs to the soles of his feet. He could feel something pouring out of himself. He'd noticed it before, occurring in direct proportion to the amount of traffic and light on the road: the less there was of each, the better he felt. It was almost as if he were floating, and he imagined the car once again disappearing around him—leaving him in a sitting position, hands working minute adjustments on invisible controls, spinning silently down the dark, empty road.

He was reminded of his father, who had told him more than once that they came from a people who'd had no aristocracy and no clergy. Somehow, Leen daydreamed, this was analogous to no people and no lights. "Our people lived in darkness and isolation but nobody complained," his father often said, making no apparent distinction between his own childhood on the farm and a pagan barbarian culture two thousand years past. Leen could never quite understand what he meant, but it always quickened his blood to hear his father talk like that. He may not have been a farmer, but he was incontestably a world class mistruster of authority.

With a surprisingly strong shudder he looked at the passenger seat; it was as if his father were traveling with him, lit faintly against the deepening twilight by the dashboard instruments and the glowing bowl of his supernatural pipe. But he was not. Not anymore he wasn't. A Nixon man to the very end. How could that have been? It made no sense—didn't seem possible given what he knew about his father and what he knew about Nixon. Maybe he would have come around. Maybe he would end up a tyrannical reactionary. His mother had pictures of him on the mantel—one in his grandfather's lap, maybe a year into life, wearing a natty little cap that said "I LIKE IKE!" and another, wearing a lime-green Nehru jacket and a "NIXON'S THE ONE!" button—that suggested Leen was now a half-breed renegade. The whole business was ghastly. Oh for a beakerful of the warm south, he mused, in the cool and peopleless north. The road rose and fell over the mounds and hills of debris the glaciers had left behind them as they retreated.

11

Leen had a busy schedule ahead of him, full of meetings with everybody from the mayor to a rank-and-file iron-worker, men and women to whom he was not a stranger and who either needed or wanted to talk to him, and yet he continued to feel uneasy. Lying on the bed in his motel room, he read the letter Leah had given him on parting, asking him to use the time away from her to think clearly about their marriage. A copy of that letter, carefully redacted at Leah Le Blanc's request, follows: *Something has changed—I see it only now—in the way you perceive people. That one crucial remove from which you have apparently been acting all your life now seems to be in the employ of everybody you know, everybody you speak to in the course of business. If I understand you correctly, they all appear quite plainly to be "going through the motions" (your words) with you, pretending to be who you think they are (who they think you think they are) and pretending that you are who you think you are (who they think you think you are), and so on. Writing it out like this of course makes it sound unmistakably insane, a textbook case of paranoia, but while I am convinced you need help, I don't think you are insane. No. You are just getting what you've asked for and it isn't what you thought it would be. This sense of remoteness is in a way a kind of confirmation that you are, after all, really and truly acting, acting in almost exactly the way actors on stage do, surrounded by characters who cannot or will not think for themselves, who act in fear of the director or the author and cannot or will not even act unless catalyzed by someone outside the theater and completely unafraid, unbound by the usual, invisible, intractable constraints, free of the tether whose length and strength he knows perfectly, to the psychological centimeter, because he measures it a hundred times a day—"the bondage," as his friend the quotable novelist once put it, "of the appropriate," the negotiated, agreed-on, and acceptable, the unactionable, the demonstrably legal, the safe, the cautious, the experienced, effective, and efficient response to anger, violence, and fear. And yet: absolutely committed to your lines as you once memorized and understood them, to the arc of the drama as it was revealed to you, long ago, in a room you can no longer place in the city, where you rehearsed and argued and laughed with real people who cared about you, loved you, and who you in turn loved.*

12

At first he thought he was dreaming. Then he believed himself in the bed of a woman he evidently knew but couldn't see well enough to recognize. *Had it been Leah?* Head clearing, he got up and looked out the window of the motel room, holding the heavy curtain aside as if he were afraid of being seen. Across the highway, at a place the men called Scab City—an old building that had been snatched up by a group of Canadian opportunists, who renovated it and charged exorbitant rents to the out-of-state workers pouring into the town—an automobile burned fantastically in the night. Reflective stripes on the coats of the firemen stood out in the headlights of an endless parade of passing cars, and a glistening silver arcing torrent of water slammed into the burning car, as if it were all some kind of fountain, an installation of postmodern art.

He felt as if something in him—not his *self* necessarily—had been summoned to appear the next morning, and slept, accordingly, almost not at all. His worries and excitement became alpha wave reveries of improbable but therefore soothing connection and broken connection. Just before dawn the mysterious woman returned to his dreams, but he didn't think it was Leah. He didn't know who she was, couldn't see her, didn't want to move, as she kissed his back for what seemed like hours. Rousing himself not long after dawn, he was met at the door of his room by a warm breeze. He came to believe that it had been Leah after all, but could not understand why he had been unable to recognize her.

The dreams had been so charged with eros—with a desire for self-preservation and sexual pleasure so over-blown he thought he could feel life ebbing and flowing with each cycle of breath—that he felt not only summoned now but possessed—or rather that the world that summoned him had been transformed, in the stricter electrical sense: the same armature of support, the same lines of transmission, but dangerously amplified power. Everything carried the charge.

The breeze too seemed to have become more dense and strong without increasing its velocity—as if its source and destination were somewhere in the earth. It was unseasonally warm, balmy almost, given the lateness of the fall and the latitude, all but a handful of leaves left on most trees, some still strangely bright, faintly electrified too. He walked to the restaurant where his first meetings were scheduled with half an erection. It was called Nancy's

Place, and Nancy was in fact its owner and proprietor. She was in her sixties, round, short, pretty, voluptuous, and had long been an activist and organizer in the far north—mainly on behalf of poor women. Both brothers and her father had been representatives in the state House, and she had herself been a Koochiching County commissioner for many years. And though the pedigree was of adversarial liberalism that went back to the earliest days of white pine lumbering and the peak of mining production in the Mesabi Iron Range, the restaurant was frequented by hard-core Chamber of Commerce types, Goldwater Republicans, and the Boise Cascade elite. It was the kind of place without which a small town lacks a heart, and no one felt unwelcome or uncomfortable there. There were old photographs of lumberjacks and politicians all over the walls, some autographed, some comically captioned. Leen's job was to arrange a more or less public meeting of representatives from the warring camps, to stage a discussion between two stout but ordinary men, a striker and and his replacement, each claiming descent from a powerful god—the same god, the god that promised food and clothing, a warm house, and a happy childhood—but stripped of armor, weaponry, and divine inspiration, wearing only the dirty overalls and windbreakers.

Leen asked Nancy how things were.

"Things are very bad."

"I saw the car on fire."

"Did you know that there was a man in that car?"

"No, I did not know that."

"He got out before it exploded."

"I'm relieved to hear that."

"Look over there in the corner—no, underneath the two-man saw."

Leen saw the mayor of the town, who appeared to be lost in thought.

"He's been up all night," said Nancy. "And he's been drinking."

Leen walked over to say hello. The mayor declined to acknowledge him, but a man Leen did not recognize told him to go fuck himself, along with his candidate and his party. The mayor said now, now, now, apparently to the wall of the booth, and Leen grinned and said he was willing to bet the other man would feel differently when election day rolled around. Then he winked. Back at the counter, Nancy bitterly derided the idea of peace talks, characterizing it as a stunt.

"Nancy, allow me to disagree with you very strongly here. This is a genuine effort to bring people who can't stand each other back to the place where they can stand each other. Nothing could be more basic to the candidate's principles, and his principles direct him absolutely. Look, this guy is really different. He's the real thing. He makes no distinction between what we'll call professional politics and what we'll call grassroots activism. He does what he thinks is right, regardless of so-called political consequences—which in truth are just the consequences of human activity, nothing more, nothing less, and therefore susceptible to further episodes of human activity—and one thing that is always always always right is standing with working people, actually, physically, and verifiably on the picket line holding a sign, when Big Business gets too big for its breeches, when it becomes tyrannical and—"

"*Wife?*" Nancy cut him off with the subdued intensity of a loan officer. "*Daughter?*"

"Both well."

"*Good,*" she said, appearing to relax. "Good. Good."

"You heard about Judge Doty's decision in favor of the Minnesota Milk Producers Assocation?"

"Yes, I did. Leah must be very pleased."

"She was ecstatic, certainly. For maybe a day. Then she got scared. She's in D.C. again. Last time, deposing Tom, Dick, and Harry. Now she's talking face-to-face with the secretary of agriculture himself."

"*You must be very proud of her.*"

"Yes, she's very able, very confident when she needs to be. Knows how to handle people. I like to watch her speak. No histrionics—just a sure hand and a steady voice."

"And your daughter?"

"Lucy's great. She's quite a character. Just got her driver's license."

"Oh my."

"Yes. Celebrated the granting of that privilege by driving to Las Vegas. I guess she was running away. But she was quite amiable about it. Spends a lot of time under a railroad bridge with her alarmingly-barbered, chained-up, jackbooted friends. Swears she will go and live there one day. I asked her if she wouldn't miss her bathroom and she said no, proved it by not taking a shower for six months. She has no interest in—not even contempt for—our politics, our liberal do-gooding. She won't finish high school. But still I admire her. I marvel at her and I can't wait to see what she'll do next. She's got a good mind. And it's all her own."

Nancy looked at Leen, guardedly, suspiciously, disapprovingly—it could have been veiled approval, too, or tenative neutrality—he had no idea what her look was supposed to imply. He knew she dealt with—had seen and known and worked with—a lot of young women in prison, halfway houses, programs, desperate circumstances of every kind. And for some reason he didn't want to talk about Lucy to her. He underscored the amiability that characterized everything Lucy did. Nancy picked up his dishes and stood before him for a long moment while the tableware of others clinked and scraped and tapped melodically around the restaurant, and the espresso machine piped in the distance, like a chamber organ providing a very high ground note.

"Things are bad, you said," Leen ventured after a while of this.

"Oh they're a lot worse than bad."

"I see."

"Have you ever spent any time in California?"

Despite Leah's having been born and raised in Los Angeles, and despite the continuing presence there of a good deal of her extended family, Leen had never been to California. He was vaguely ashamed of this, but admitted it was so. The connection to conditions in a sawmill town on the borders of Minnesota and Ontario was not immediately clear, but Nancy commenced a monologue that was clearly a product of frayed nerves.

"I have never seen such clean cars. My sister lives near Riverside, and I tried it in my midforties. It struck me as neurotic, like a fetish, how clean they were kept. Museum quality. It made me ill. What is it about California anyway? I had this fixed notion of California. I don't know how I came to it. But the main features were Johnny Carson's Hollywood, and the Beach Boys." Nancy now seemed to be trying very hard to make pleasant small talk. "You know, that good-natured irony that Carson infused everything with. Even the biggest stars seemed like regular people. Pals. And sports cars. Convertibles on the Pacific Highway. And of course Xanadu and San Francisco. But it's not like that. At least not in San Bernardino or Long Beach. Not at all. I suppose I'm just being naive in a way that would bore me to tears in any other circumstance. But it was just these . . . gigantic, immaculate pickup trucks. Driven by mean, drunken good old boys who only looked like the Beach Boys. No, listen, there is a point to this, I can see the look in your eyes. We're in Koochiching County, Minnesota. Frostbite Falls. But whatever was going on out there in California, it—"

"The aerospace industry."

"—it, yes, I understand that. But—"

"It happened in Pittsburgh, it happened in Detroit, it happened to farmers—"

"*Yes. Yes. I know that. But it's come here.* No: I don't mean the raw deal. I don't just mean the jobs are gone. Because they're not gone. They've just been discounted and cheapened and I'm sorry, I'm sorry I'm sorry sorry sorry—" Nancy was waving at Leen now and he didn't understand why—he thought she might be anticipating some remark from him and angrily dismissing it—until he heard the sob. One bark escaped her and then she caught herself. She stopped abruptly, held herself very still, passed her hands over her face and smiled at Leen, tears streaming down her cheeks. "I hate them," she said, smiling brilliantly, defiantly.

"You hate them?"

"I do! Oh my GOD how I've come to hate them!"

"Well," Leen said sternly, "of course you do. We all do. Who exactly are we talking about . . .?"

"*The men in the pickups!*" shouted Nancy, loudly enough for Leen to hold his hands up in a plea for caution. "And their WOMEN! Those insufferable, loudmouthed, ignorant, selfish, greedy HARRIDANS they're married to!"

Leen sat quietly while conversations around them were carefully taken up and resumed.

"Are you talking about the scabs?" he asked in a strange murmur that was partly a wish to soothe Nancy and partly a stomach-churning, throat-constricting surge of anxiety. He was aware that large portions of Southern California were really just a Mediterranean-style extension of the Deep South, and wondered if they were simply talking about rednecks and other forms of white trash.

"I am *not* talking about the scabs!" Nancy whispered harshly.

13

Nancy leaned across the counter and put her face very close to Leen's. She had become like Carrie Nation in her sudden wrath, like a mother in a nightmare. Whatever he was planning to do up here, she said in a voice now strangely deep and slow, she wanted no part of it. And then she whispered again: she begged him to please not try to have sexual intercourse with any of her waitresses. He offered a vaguely stricken, strangely sorrowful disclaimer, repeating her name several times, but she held her hand up like a traffic cop, silencing him, then left— only to return distractedly for the dishes, smiling ruefully, as if—almost—to say *oh don't mind me*.

14

Leen walked toward the door. Reaching it, he realized he hadn't left a tip. The space at the counter where he'd been sitting seemed much farther away than it could have been. In fact, he could no longer see it. His heart was pounding in his throat and he was visibly trembling. He laughed out loud, as if to demonstrate the lightness of his heart, and nearly slapped his forehead as he dashed back, nearly blind with panic, to his seat with the tip. He was certainly afraid but his attitude toward fear was not at all ordinary. Confronted with a properly frightening stimulus and ordinary physiological responses, Leen would, rather than flee or fight, attempt to teach himself a lesson. Fundamental to such attempts was the old theatrical belief that the mind would follow the body: slapping one's knees was actually conducive of laughter—and even if it failed, it was a helpful cue for the audience. This practice had its source in an inarticulate but healthy Buddhist-like desire to accept things as they are with a calm spirit, but had become over time punitive and perverse in Leen. By forcing himself to act unafraid, he only deepened his fear and, in effect, ritualized it. Violence was the only possible conclusion— which, because it made him feel so good, so spirited and consequential, began to call out for its own renewal.

15

Leen's retreat from sensibility was not swift and orderly— as it had been when he smashed up the family car eight years earlier—but the same process was under way. In a very short while, less than a year, he would come to think of his life as unremittingly devoted to fraud and conceit, of himself as a remorseless bully, jerk, swindler, and coward. (He quotes another party when he says this, but insists the phrase has always had a roundness and simplicity that he can't say he doesn't find compelling.) But all that was to come. Grinning falsely but with a kind of hope, counting out bills there at the table, he felt something like what Rip van Winkle must have felt: for the whole twenty years of his adult life had been to him but as one night. If he thought he had been dreaming, he knew he was most definitely no longer doing so. He had been awakened. He felt that most strongly: growing evidence and increasing belief that whatever had seemed to be going on before—the transformation wrought by Leah's love and the ensuing fairy tale—he had been asleep and was now, consequently, awake. He supposed there was a moment of true panic when he didn't know exactly where he was, an overwhelmingly irrational rejection of observable reality when he was convinced his life was in danger, but he was so thoroughly accustomed to winging it, to politics, that he transformed that fear—as he put his water glass on top of the tip—into a thrill, a self-aggrandizing interpretation of his impulses as essentially those of a daredevil.

16

He stumbled so forthrightly through the ruts and mud of Nancy's parking lot that he must have appeared drunk, and drove with shrieking angels of shame in one ear and bellowing devils of defiance in the other and a great weight of darkened, imperfect self-knowledge on his shoulders to the other side of town and the Bronislaw "Bronko" Nagurski Museum. Nagurski was a native son— born across the river in Ontario—proudly believed by the town and noted historians of football to have been the greatest player ever. The museum is attached to the Koochiching County Historical Museum, in Smokey Bear Park, which features a statue of Smokey Bear (twenty-six feet high, with two cubs included) and what was for a short while the world's tallest thermometer (twenty-two feet high, with a digital display at its base). His plan, arranged while he was still in the Twin Cities, was to have a rank-and-file striker and a scab meet on the more or less neutral ground of a football museum, exchange views, shake hands, get his candidate's name associated with the event, and secure commitments for another such event, at which the candidate would himself arbitrate. He was met, however, at the door by curators of both the Nagurski and the county museums, a representative from the state parks, a communications officer from BE&K, a local staffer from the Republican whose district in Congress this was, and, unbelievably, the county sheriff.

As he took them in, it was not entirely lost on him that, whatever else these men might be, whatever else they wanted—from him, from themselves, from the world— they were first of all a committee, just another group representing various other groups, gathered as a means to an end—he had to believe—that did not necessarily exclude mutual satisfaction. This was the mechanism of mechanisms, the clockwork by which all concerned could regulate democracy and predict compassion.

But he saw he was going to lose this one and he couldn't manage it. He couldn't bear it. He felt weak and tired and nearly crazy. He lost his temper almost immediately, but it wouldn't have mattered if he'd not: acts of hostility were being perpetrated all over town, on a daily basis; a kind of gang warfare had erupted and the level of violence was escalating rapidly. Because he was nervous and unbalanced—and he supposed giving way, already, to real panic (what he'd felt at Nancy's having been nothing more than a lighting of a fuse)—he shouted, very loudly, what he imagined would be an appeal to reason: did not the fear of worsening violence make the idea of peace talks thrillingly imperative? They trooped awkwardly into the Bronko Nagurski Conference Room, took turns speaking briefly and tersely. The short answer was no, fear of worsening violence made the idea of peace talks neither thrilling nor imperative. Fear of worsening violence did not open up new vistas for weary hunters and gatherers of peace, as Leen insisted with crazy eloquence. It moved no one in any way except toward increasingly truculent intransigence, hardened hearts, and irrational antipathy. The park and museum people could not use federal or state facilities for such a political stunt, the Boise Cascade people had established numerous channels and means of communication and shown an unflagging willingness to negotiate until the cows came home and all the smoke-filled back rooms of the state were filled to capacity and beyond. The sheriff said he did not want to see volatile, popular emotions given any further excuse to be dramatized.

No, said Leen, now is exactly the time for all that to happen.

The Republican's staffer rolled his eyes at Leen while the others murmured disapprovingly and looked away, embarrassed or pretending to be embarrassed, he couldn't tell which.

"Don't do that," he said, much more quietly.

"Don't do what exactly?" asked the staffer, loudly.

"Roll your eyes."

"I'll roll whatever I feel like rolling."

"Sure, it's a free country, no question, I'm just asking you, don't."

The staffer took a step toward him, out of the little crowd, and pointed his finger at Leen. "*Are you—*"

"Yes!" Leen shouted. "I'M THREATENING YOU! IF THAT FINGER GETS ANY CLOSER TO ME I WILL BREAK IT OFF AND SHOVE IT UP YOUR ASS!"

He knew he had effectively removed himself from the campaign in that moment, that he had sabotaged a long-cherished dream, and that the repercussions would be uncontrollable and therefore in all likelihood disastrous—much more so than the car crash—but there is a moment of chemical reaction, of psychological sound as brief and clear as a twig snapping underfoot on a cold and still winter night, during which the remorseless begetting of hatred from hatred, violence from violence, fear from fear . . . feels very much like pure joy.

17

As he made his way triumphantly from the lobby of the Nagurski, Leen heard the staccato *beep beep beep* of a car horn. Across the parking lot, near the thermometer, he saw headlights go on and off, on and off, then an arm waving from a window. He jogged over, feeling clean and happy as a junkie while the adrenaline burned. Then suddenly he felt cold and empty. The car stank of beer and cigarette butts and in it were two men, both pale, red-eyed. One, lighting a cigarette with the dash lighter, was a steward from one of the striking unions, who was going to supply the charismatic but typical rank-and-filer Leen was looking for, and the other, stubbing out his smoke, was a local DFL caucus chief. They were both quite young to be in such positions of responsibility, but he knew them to be as intelligent as they were ambitious, and he felt a lichenous hope bloom in his heart. They took a long drive, ending up at Nancy's. They'd been talking optimistically, even fervently, as they drove, but as soon as they came to a stop, they fell silent. Leen saw Nancy standing at the back door, and waved.

"Everybody seems on edge," he said.

"You can't go to da stinkin' grocery store without having to watch some awful catfight, ya know," said the steward, lapsing suddenly into a thick northwoods accent, so suddenly Leen turned around to grin at him, thinking he was putting it on, but saw only unfocused anxiety.

"Nancy sure doesn't seem like herself," he said. He weighed what he was about to say and found it light but sharp, provocative but not outrageous, a kind of pick-me-up. "She told me explicitly not to fuck any of her waitresses." Neither of the men replied, but the local Dem shut the engine off. "Why would she say that?" Leen asked after a while. Saying such a thing out loud was like leveling a spell or a curse on himself. The very words made him angry and ashamed, but not in the ordinary way: it was like hand over hand, climbing a rope suspended over an abyss.

The steward cleared his throat. "I don't know. I *do* know some guys came in here a few days ago and told her she'd better not be seen serving scabs, and she says she's seen some . . . *aggressive driving* that she can't account for. I also know that some of our guys are mad as hell, and that some of them are lunkheads, and that most of us are tired of taking shit. But I can tell you this, and this is the last thing I know: *none of this is coming from us.*"

18

Leen entered the dark, noisy, stinking interior of the Bear Grease Bar and Grill in International Falls, Minnesota, on the evening of October 28, 1996. The tavern was unusually crowded. It was hard to get from one place to another, and it stank incredibly of flatulence, as if everyone had let loose at once. Beneath an electric sign advertising a beer that had once been brewed in the state ("from the land of sky blue waters," the jingle had gone, sung to the sound of tom-toms), on which a crystalline stream appeared to flow through a sylvan glade, he saw the mayor of the town—a man who had worked in the paper mill forty years, both as a union man and as part of management—the publisher of the local newspaper, and a reporter whom he knew very well, from the Minneapolis paper. He looked at them: all three were bald, their skulls glowing with reflected light, rich blues and greens from the beer sign. The publisher asked him if he was happy now, and Leen replied with mild, frightened, forgettable sarcasm.

"*Ah fuck you,*" said the publisher, smiling strangely, as if perhaps he were tasting the venom of his words. The mayor looked away and the reporter waited brazenly. The publisher adjusted his glasses and maintained the poisoned grin. Leen pointed out that the candiate, along with the unions, was in fact opposed to the strike and was asking strikers to return to work. The table erupted in violent laughter. The reporter took Leen by the elbow through the crowd to another table, from which drinkers were rising. He'd spent the afternoon trying to sleep, but the room felt like a cage and his thoughts were ridiculous, petty, finally incoherent. His blood seethed and the ticking of his heart was like drops of water falling with clocklike regularity, from a great height, on his skull. He'd risen from the bed, tried to call both Leah and Lucy but connected with neither, drove to Nancy's where he tried again from a phone booth, bought a cup of coffee to go, and tried to apologize to Nancy, who seemed not to know what he was talking about. Now he was picking up some steam again. He had thought and thought and thought and come up with so little in the way of consolation that thinking seemed sick, abusive, useless, and only the picking up of steam and eventual release of it could bring him any sense of peace. That such a conclusion made no sense was only further evidence that the time for thinking was done.

"They defy *everybody*, see," he said, trying to talk his way calmly through it, as if the reporter were a therapist, "and when I say everybody I mean *even themselves*. They stage a wildcat strike. What is a wildcat strike? One that's red in tooth and claw? It's invisible and meaningless and they know it. They become bitter and maybe ruthless in some relative way. These are guys who will sell the house, the car, the fishing boat, everything, and just keep standing there, forty below zero, until they lose it all. Losing it all becomes the goal, becomes a source of pride, a source, perhaps paradoxically, of energy. They're willing it to take it—take everybody and everything—to the beginning. Which is the same as the end."

The reporter regarded him with a judiciously critical deadpan for a long stretch of seconds, then asked, "Aren't most of the wildcatters, though, this is what I—correct me if—nonlocals, from as far away as Duluth or even farther? Who gave up immediately and went home to other jobs?"

"Duluth is local. Alabama is not local. The U.P. is local. Texas is not local."

The reporter sat back and smiled. He looked to Leen like a different man altogether now that he was no longer lit by the beer sign. Had Leen betrayed a lurking hatred of Alabama and Texas? "It seems to me," said the reporter loudly, "that the unions are plainly and simply being greedy, standing in the way of progress here, a rejuvenated town. BE&K wants to employ people, and the unions are saying fuck you, aren't they? Our way or no way?"

"No, that's not right," Leen said with feigned meekness of spirit.

"How is it then?" demanded the reporter with feigned (Leen thought) belligerence. Then he laughed. Leen decided suddenly that he was tired of talking to morons and slid out of the booth. "You said something about bitter and ruthless?" the reporter went on. "Relatively ruthless?"

"Whatever."

"Good guys and bad guys, eh?"

"My, aren't you sophisticated."

The reporter winked at Leen and Leen winked back.

A block-featured man with huge arms, a barrel chest, and spindly little legs appeared next to him. He wore a thick mustache, a cap advertising Shakespeare fishing reels, and an ironworkers union windbreaker. He regarded Leen impassively. "Where's da udder guy?" he finally asked. The union steward bobbed up over his shoulder and said something Leen couldn't make out in the din. He recognized the ironworker as someone he'd seen in the local paper. The man continued to regard him impassively, though his face was reddening alarmingly. A tall, thin, gaunt man, also wearing a mustache, droopier, wispier, like a catfish's whiskers, and a cap advertising fishing gear from Bass Pro Shops, appeared in a widening gap between two groups of people. A photographer began to take pictures. Leen felt he had enough steam up to feel like the flash was a strobe light. He couldn't remember anybody's name, so he flipped through his pocket notepad while trying to get the attention of a waitress and faces flashed on and off in the darkness. Then she was there, pretending to be perky and full of common sense and he had some names back. He introduced the striker and the scab, himself, the reporter from Minneapolis, and the mayor. The drinks, he told them all, would be on the Democratic-Farmer-Labor party.

19

A waitress leaned toward him and he ordered another shot of bourbon and a beer. A man, stern-looking and well if casually dressed, older, silver-haired, military-clean, crossed between him and the diplomats. The silver-haired man caught the scab's eye and sat down on the other side of Leen's little table. Leen waited for him to ask if it was all right, and when he didn't, said, "No, I don't mind." The silver-haired man ignored him. Leen thought he knew him, and that the man in turn knew him, but he couldn't make the connection. Had he been at the Nagurski? It couldn't have been. Perhaps sitting in one of the cars outside the museum? The waitress came with his beer and shot and he drank them quickly. "Looks like a stage set, doesn't it?" he asked loudly, leaning across the table. "Like they're rehearsing a play?" The ironworker was leaning forward across their booth table, arms and eyes open wide, Nordic face reddening, making points so big nobody could miss them, even if nobody could hear them. The tall man, the scab, was doing a sleepy border ruffian, playing the cards he'd been dealt, lethal, biding his time. Leen cast a stagey look at the men, then came back with exaggerated head-swinging focus to his table companion, who continued to ignore him.

"They're running their lines like they don't know where they're supposed to stand yet, what props they're going to pick up and put down, like they don't quite know who they are yet."

"Excuse me," said the silver-haired man. "Do you mind?"

"Do I mind?" The silver-haired man stared at him and he stared back. The ironworker and the tall man continued their big exasperated point-making and lethal time-biding. The sense of a play within a play within a play within a play was suddenly intolerable. Leen laughed so loudly that the silver-haired man had to look away. Leen caught the waitress by the arm and ordered again, indicating he would buy for the other guy at the table as well. He guessed that the silver-haired man was somebody rather high up in BE&K security, and that he had in fact seen him with the communications officer at some point. He guessed everybody was spoiling for a fight. Thinking so made him feel sentimentally sober. Another wave of shame washed over him, then simple embarrassment, followed by a wish to be nonviolent and calm, but powerful and impressive. The din of bad country music and shouted conversations whirled around him, the blue and green beer lights worked their magic, soothing and exciting at once, helping him imagine, more and more perfectly and less and less clearly, the inward cosmic design: two heavenly tracks revolving around an unmoving center, himself at three points simultaneously, at the center, breathing and watching, circling slowly on the inner ring, chopping wood and carrying water, and on the high-speed outer ring, a blur of motion, action, consequence.

He felt distinctly unliked here, perhaps for the first time in his life, and, for better or worse, unlikable. This thought cheered him with improbable force and efficiency.

20

If people of spirit and principle (Leen thought, sitting on the bed in his motel room staring at the phone with his head in his hands), if people of intelligence and strength and compassion do not act decisively when . . . when . . . he tried to remember how the I Ching used to put it . . . when the great water must be crossed . . . then all is lost. Rule will be by pack, packs formed of the maddest dogs on the planet, bad dogs, the only bad dogs: men.

He thought this over and over in various keys and tempi, wanting very much to call Leah and talk to her but knowing it was the last thing he should do, being, as he was, incontrovertibly drunk.

21

A very cold breeze met Leen at the door the next morning. He realized he hadn't packed anything for winter weather, and winter weather was clearly coming. He walked against it all the way to the union hall, where a disturbingly large number of men had already gathered. He was met coolly. No one understood why he was there. He was too little too late. Leen attempted feigned astonishment at their ingratitude, but couldn't bring it off. The show was over. Last night was closing night, and it had been absurd, but at least it would be in the Minneapolis and Saint Paul papers, for whatever that might turn out to be worth. Over and over again, as he milled about in the general aimless circulation of men and emotion, he said he was there because the candidate cared, the DFL cared, and because the union cared, even if they were like family members who were too close and couldn't express their true feelings. There was, he asserted, a difference between an official and largely political stance, and the heart and soul of the liberal, democratic, and union leadership—not to mention those many grassroots organizations that were banding together and in whom they should feel nothing but solid confidence. He reminded them how overanxious they had been to sign the contract that dangled the expansion and new paper machine as a guarantee they

could all retire where they were and live comfortably until they died—but which, the union had counseled, held
hidden traps along with the clearly stated wage cuts. We
wanted you, he said, to stop *then* and think. We want you
now, he said, to end the strike. We want you, he said, to
avenge yourselves in the next round of negotiations. The
cumulative effect, however, of this oddly deliberate and
aphoristic glad-handing seemed only to be a fanning of
the smoldering fire. One by one, the men grew louder
and louder, each struggling to make himself understood
to his likewise struggling mate. Then in twos and threes
and fours, they came to Leen—the only outsider in the
room—with that mixture—he thought—of defiant anger
and troubled guilt they might bring to a representative of
a church in a time of social tumult. As he tried to read between the lines and put two and two together, he became
more and more excited, troubled, and distracted—as if he
had forgotten a great or terrible thing that he might recall
if the men would only let him be for a second. He found
himself making big, placatory gestures, as if he were again
on a stage, but this time in no intimate supper-club setting, rather in an auditorium seating many thousands.
The speech and motion of the men around him, and his
own as well, began to speed up. The more deliberately he
tried to take hold of himself, the faster it all seemed. Then
some important firewall in his mind was breached and he
felt as if he were in a hive, the nether reaches of which
were burning, the din of voices a high-pitched and ominously loud droning, the scope and pace and nature of

the work going on around him on a different scale of time and space altogether. He could see it, he could hear it, but he could not—and this was as painful as it was ominous to sense—participate. He felt ill at ease in a way he could not control with the usual methods, which had been coming apart at the seams for days now—years, according to Leah's letter—and when he saw a bottle of whiskey with a stack of paper cups next to it in a back room, he helped himself. It was too early in the morning—but a drink of forbidden, dangerous alcohol would be bracing in a way he could not devalue. It would put him back in the room with everybody else. The stomach-deep stink of cigarettes and perhaps fear, the nauseating green paint of the cement block walls, the fluorescent lighting and the uncomfortable plastic chairs, the coffee stains and the scuff marks and the muddy boot-prints from a day gone by on the cracked tile of the floor—all this would come quickly to seem good and proper. A drink was like a tool, and he needed to fix something. A drink was like a light and a tool. He would find the thing that was broken and fix it. His days on the campaign were numbered, but he could at least fix this thing, this leak, this short circuit, the high-pitched whine and the banging and clattering of gears shorn of teeth, this murkiness or whatever it was that rendered good faith and common sense, enduring institutions of democracy and ancient rites of negotiation, useless, ridiculous, insulting. A drink would be like a shop in the garage at home, even if home is where they hated a man the most.

22

Two men stood waiting for Leen to finish his second drink. *Where had they come from?* He eyed them frankly but professionally over the rim of his cup, watching them watch him, while he drank quite a lot of whiskey, both because it felt good and because he knew it would impress the men. Both of them were tall, blond, blue-eyed, heavy, with big bellies hanging out over their belts, but not quite obese. Both wore ball caps advertising fishing equipment that were too small for their immense red-faced heads. One wore a mustache that covered his mouth, the other a beard that covered his face.

When Leen set his cup down and performed the grimace of satisfaction by strong drink, the two drew rather too near for comfort, and poured themselves drinks. For all the provocativeness of their posture and resemblance to trolls, they struck him as orphans, waifs—lost and confused, certainly, but kindhearted and wishing only for a chance to do something well and helpful. The idea, which had also instantly occurred to him, that they were representatives of a radical faction, even a secret society, he dismissed as unworthy. They were drunk, swaying already, and smelling strongly of it, but Leen had climbed aboard and settled in for an exciting trip on the scenic route.

He poured another round for the three of them. "Gentlemen," he said, "I think everything's going to work out okay. I really admire what you're doing up here. It's a mess but our way of life is going to—"

"We need to talk to you," said the man with the mustache.

"Outside."

They spoke abruptly but, he judged, apologetically. They went down a hallway stacked on both sides with cardboard boxes, head high. The door at the end of the hallway had a window in it, which seemed at first to be translucent, filtering luminous silver light, but that turned out to be clear. They approached the door, the trolls on either side, as if escorting him, meaty shoulders turned inward and scraping the boxes so that there was a steady susurration of flannel on cardboard. Stepping outside, Leen saw that it was snowing, just a few flakes dancing down to the rutted dirt of a parking lot and melting. It was early for snow, but not that early this far north, and he made too much of it. He knew he was making too much of it, going on and on about *snow* for Christ's sake, so when the faux lumberjack with the grubby infestation of beard walloped him upside the head, his first thought was that it was the unintentionally powerful equivalent of a slug on the arm, a kidding reproof. He turned dizzily toward the place where the blow had come from and took a second from somewhere far away. Dazed, he allowed himself to be struck a few more times with that kind of force that is not so much startlingly frightening as numbingly inarguable. Dazed, he was stuffed into a trunk and, dazed, found the cool rattling bouncing banging darkness not altogether unpleasant. He was not afraid—it was too preposterous a situation for fear or even serious concern. He wasn't angry, and—he checked again—wasn't frightened. It was like being in a mobile cave. The tires whined like turbines deep in his head and gravel roared like rain against the underside of the trunk. He banged his head repeatedly against the lid and it felt good, as if sense could in fact be introduced in this way. It was like insistent knocking on a door late at night that he had special dispensation not to answer. He was entering a world of moral freedom and mob violence. As the journey progressed, the idea became more and more thrilling. Consequently he became less and less able to think clearly. By the time the car ground fishtailing to a halt, and he'd rolled to the front of the trunk and back, he was paralyzed—having gone, effectively, around the world in the opposite direction of fear only to arrive at its backside. When the trunk was opened on a painfully bright snow-filled sky and several ski-masked heads, it was as if he had surprised fear by coming at it from the rear. It spun and regarded him angrily.

"I'm on your side," he said with the rehearsing actor's lack of conviction.

"Whatever," said one man.

"He doesn't have a blindfold on," said another.

"*Well, put one on him,*" squealed the first. "Jesus fucking *Christ.*"

"I don't have one!"

Leen could see rosy little lips bunched up in the mouth holes of the ski masks and remembered building snow forts and snowmen with his friends—of whom there had seemed to be a thousand. Where had they all gone? Had the nature of friendship changed? Had he become unfriendly in the course of his pursuit of broad-based bipartisan happiness? Everyone, friend and foe alike, seemed to be suffering in the way the first man in the ski mask was suffering. Friendship was no longer possible.

"I'm on your side," he repeated, making a gesture as if he wished to keep the noise down. The men repudiated this idea confusedly and obscenely.

Again he made a pedantic gesture. The first man told him to close his eyes and commanded one of the other men, peevishly, to make sure he kept them shut. This man swung his head around and stared passionately at Leen, his eyes huge in their double-stitched sockets. Then they hustled him into a house. Despite their obviously frayed nerves and strained voices, they were rather polite as they marched him up the walk. All concerned were beginning the process of identifying with each other. Soon, Leen imagined, they would be drinking and joking. The violence would be sudden and apologetic, or perfunctory and wan. These guys seemed like hapless idiots, so it could go any of several different ways. He was quite sure he wasn't dealing with union men, but the affiliations and goals of his captors remained mysterious. He suspected *posse comitatus*, Aryan Nation militiamen, taking him as a representative of a repressive government, but it was also possible they were in the employ of whatever covert organization or organizations were actually responsible for the breaking of the unions, trying to pass themselves off as deadly radicals within the ranks of the already unpredictably reckless wildcatters.

A strip of cloth was found to blind him, and he was seated in what he believed to be the kitchen. Something like a day passed. Waking after a nap on the floor next to the table, he smelled gasoline, and assumed gasoline was the liquid he could hear being poured from one container to another, and that Molotov cocktails were being prepared. The man doing the pouring breathed heavily, not as if winded by cheerful exercise, he thought, but as if laboring to stay ahead of panic. Glass bottles clinked. Then he heard a slap, a steady gurgling, glugging, the respiratory-like flexing of plastic, and the loud, unmistakable sound of liquid splashing from countertop to floor.

The man cursed so suddenly and loudly that Leen jumped to his feet, hitting his head on a shelf and knocking something from it that crashed and broke on the floor around him. The man continued to curse violently, uncontrollably, until at last he seemed hysterical and entirely incoherent. There was a sweeping sound and then a crash of glass and weeping. Leen was spattered with gasoline and bits of powdered glass.

He pulled the blindfold off and scrambled awkwardly away from the table, banging his leg painfully on one of its legs. He found himself next to a door and tried it, rattling the knob back and forth and tugging at it, thinking it was not locked but merely stuck. Tongue becoming heavy and unwieldy in his mouth, he fashioned grunting noises that mostly came out his nose, and slammed his shoulder again and again against the door. He stopped only when he realized the other man was still in the kitchen and sobbing. Leen leaned back in amazement and wonder against the door and it opened. He stepped outside.

Nobody seemed to be about. The snow was still light and melting on the ground. He looked left and right, and saw some traffic on the road to the left and walked, limping a little, toward it. A sign at the junction conveniently pointed the way back to town, and he settled into a long, slow, steady stride. Some indeterminate time into the walk, a fire engine roared past. He turned to watch it and saw a plume of smoke above the treetops, more or less over the place where he thought he'd just been. Quite a while later, it came back the other way, siren and horn again blasting, lights striking him even in daylight like blows. Wobbling in its slipstream, he continued to make his way toward town.

23

It turned out that he was quite a ways out of town, and he walked past his motel in swiftly darkening autumnal twilight. It had grown colder and the snow had thickened and begun to collect. In his flannel shirt and windbreaker, he was frankly cold. The falling flakes held the last of the light and glowed on the ground. Smoke from several fires in town had been visible for most of his journey, and he was cold enough to want to be warmed by them. His head still ached from the banging it had taken, but the cold felt good on his face. Several chartered buses stood silent and empty along the street. They offered no evidence of who their passengers might have been, nor to what end they had been transported. He stood on the sidewalk and found that in the lapse of those blindfolded few hours, he could not remember what the men looked like who'd slugged him, nor the man, a different man, he thought, who'd failed to make the Molotov cocktails. He realized he couldn't remember because he didn't care. His mind was elsewhere: was this not the perfect time and place to be idealistic and principled and compassionate? If so,

why did he find such things so perfectly beyond reach?
He heard shouting in the wind and began to walk toward
it. A pickup passed him going very fast, tried to make the
turn to the street he was approaching, but didn't make it.
Tires screeching, it struck a fire hydrant a glancing blow
and went up over the curb into a brick wall, just missing a plate glass window displaying shoes. Three men fell
out of the cab—one after another, the second falling on
top of the first, the third atop the second—and ran away.
Were they the same three men? He thought they might be,
and he was quite sure that if he'd had a gun he would have
fired on them—that did not seem beyond him. A group of
people appeared around another corner down the block.
They ran toward him. They were moving quickly and right
at him, but as if they couldn't see him. He flattened himself against the storefront—fine jewelry—and they shot
past, grinning with delight or exertion or fear, he couldn't
tell which. He heard a siren and looked over his shoulder.
Nearly at the vanishing point, in a gauzy web of bare, distant branches, he made out a red light. Swiftly it was upon
him, a cop car, followed by an ambulance. The shouting
was louder, and he wished he had a warmer jacket, or a
pair of gloves. Then, as if he were in a fairy tale again, he
passed a storefront from which the plate glass had been
smashed. There for the taking was a pair of gloves. An
assortment, actually: canvas working gloves, nice leather
driving gloves, big fat down-filled mittens. Choppers,
they'd called them. *Alberta clipper coming, put your choppers
on if you're going out.* He looked at them but did not take
them. Instinctively he'd known the right thing to do—and
was overjoyed at the knowledge. Several cars and pickups

roared past, as if in a high-speed convoy, bumper to bumper at sixty or more, he thought. They went through the intersection ahead, scattering groups congregated on all four corners. He was in the downtown shopping district now, and it was being, or recently had been, looted. He did not find this either terrifying or unbelievable. Down the block to his right, he heard a man shouting in a crowd that had given him a good deal of space. Leen approached and saw he was waving a gun. He was exhorting the crowd to come and steal his wares if they dared. A woman stood in the doorway of the shop—sporting goods, he saw with faint interest that might have easily become alarm—and screamed incoherently, bent nearly double in her agony. The crowd's response seemed to be amusement. Leen began to wonder if the man was actually a looter dramatizing the story of how he'd come by his weapon. He wanted the man's revolver with such a sense of righteous fervency that he actually considered knocking him down and taking it. The laughter and the screaming together were disconcerting in a way that forced him to acknowledge that he was in fact afraid—that he had been for some time. The old pedagogic habit asserted itself. It was like breaking through a paper banner at the high school football game. He was out on the playing field now, more or less alone, moms and dads and brothers and sisters and friends all watching him as he performed the rites of order, decency, and justice.

He continued to make his way to the mill. It was full dark now, and colder. The snow was falling steadily, and his feet worked like little shovels in it. If he had felt he was merely observing—say from the first blow to his head on—his recognition that fear was at work persuaded him to act at the first opportunity. He broke into a trot. That felt like the appropriate action. The years of exercise and abstinence from alcohol had restored him to fighting weight, and it felt good to run. Weighing flight and fight in repose, people often neglected to consider how fine a thing it was to run.

A crowd he (and other sources) estimated at several hundred had gathered around the mill's rather Victorian main gate, which was closed and guarded by an armed security force. Men shouted hoarsely and with a certain aimlessness; the rhythms were similar to barking—*bark bark bark* was all he could make out—but it was as if the pack had forgotten what had alarmed them. The guards were dressed in sharp-looking black fashions, with ball caps that advertised their employer. Their faces were impassive but their hands rested arrogantly, gallingly on their weapons. Then, over the barking, came the distinctive *pop pop pop* of distant firearm discharge, and the security team went to pieces. They drew their weapons and held them up next to their heads like movie stars, but milled about more or less in place like barnyard fowl in ballet tights. Several of them entered a gray midsize Ford and sped off into the heart of the mill. Several union outliers ran along the street side of the fence, followed by a single-file line of the faster runners in the crowd and then, as if the crowd were disgorging lumps of its partially digested self, bigger, more slowly-moving groups. Leen surged with them to another entrance. A pickup truck appeared down the block. He watched it approach, becoming convinced that it was the same truck he'd seen crash minutes earlier. But how could it have been? It had been broken and hissing. He got a good look at the three men in the cab as they passed close enough to run over his toes, and was now absolutely convinced for no good reason that they were the same three men. As to whether or not they were his abductors, he remained in doubt. The pickup increased its speed audibly as it neared the chain-link gate, struck it, burst the gate apart and sent it flying, and dragged several sections of the fence down on either side. Slowing almost to a stop as they cleared the part of the fence they'd driven over, Leen leapt, unaccountably, into the open bed.

Again he was swept from side to side in a metal container, banging ripe bruises and nearly falling out in the course of a four-wheel drift around a bunkhouse—one of several temporary quarters for replacement workers and their families. One of these was wholly consumed in fire. He let go of the side of the bed from which he'd been hanging, feet flying and bouncing merrily above the road as if he were a northwoods Mercury, and fell to his knees with a muffled but painful splat in the snow and mud. Men, women, and children were pouring out of the other barracks. They were moving as fast as they could, he thought, but it was only as if they were late for something. They looked annoyed and frustrated, not frightened, tripping and falling with great dignity, even though one of the men from the truck was firing his pistol overhead and screaming. Leen stood up and watched flames leap up in windows like fiery ghosts in some amusement park's haunted house. He felt as if he were dreaming again, watching the Scab City burn that first night—only two, three nights ago? Then he realized one of the scabs had been singled out and was being led off into the darkness. The third and fourth barracks were now aflame, and in that shimmering heat-distorted light he could see the pistol to the scab's baseball-capped head. Then the group disappeared—not around a corner but as if into thin air. Leen began to walk as if through water in the direction the scab had been taken. He felt better and stronger and more clearheaded with each swimming step. But by the time he reached the scene it was over. His clearheadedness was only a terrible vulnerability and the strength of his spirit—however great it may have been relative to the moment before or the years before—was easily overwhelmed and beaten down. He began shrieking for help and running but neither the motions of his legs and arms nor the sounds he was making seemed right or good in any way. At the far end of the narrow space between barracks, he saw a gray car turning away from him. He stood and shouted a strange bellowing shout, saw the taillights jump up to the brighter red, the white reverse lights come on, and then elevate slightly as the driver floored it and the car swam crazily backward toward him. Halfway down the alley, the driver forgot to turn the wheel in the opposite direction in which he wanted to go, and the car spun around, slamming into a barracks wall and knocking it down entirely, revealing the burning interior. The men in the car jumped out with their guns drawn. Leen looked down at the scab just in time to see the man's mouth form several words for which he could not find the breath to speak, working quietly, patiently, tenderly to fashion these last words, then die. Was it the man with whom he'd arranged negotiations of the night before? He couldn't tell; nobody seemed to be any-body in particular anymore.

When he looked up again, he was surrounded.

24

Though she was not yet licensed to drive, Lucy borrowed a friend's battered, unregistered, and thoroughly unreliable Econoline van and drove, in brilliant and lethal punk attire, all the way from Minneapolis to the Falls by herself. She was angry and confused and drove recklessly, poorly, at times almost comically, but with a terrible and dark sense of mission and doomed but implacable will. She thought bitterly and extravagantly of her parents and their pathetic homespun grassroots liberalism, but as she drew closer and closer to the little paper-mill town in the deep north, she began to feel on the edge of a great and strange un-derstanding, a clarity of moral vision and suddenness of belief that only the young can know, can admit and yield to. But by the time she arrived, her practical nature had asserted itself and she found herself simply embarrassed by her father's incarceration. She was ashamed of her own embarrassment as well as the earlier nunlike rapture at the approach of epiphany and now so confused that nothing of what he was trying to tell her of his own spiritual har-rowing could sink in. She washed off most of her makeup and removed the jewelry from the most grotesque pierc-ings and pressed to know the details of the arrests—he was one of a hundred and fifty men who'd been rounded up on various charges—and if anybody from the campaign or the party knew what had happened to him, but he did not want to talk about any of that. It did not seem to matter to him in any way. He wanted to talk to her about something else that was much more important, beyond cause and effect, regarding the nature of the universe and our place in it.

It was the sensation of incredible speed and immense space he'd felt as he watched the southern boy die. There was no hovering of the soul. It was as if, no longer bound by gravity, the soul shot instantly into space, overleaping all cause and all effect, back to the origins of the universe. And because Leen had been there, so close, he went a little way with it, the soul, only to fall back to Earth, slowly, weightlessly, drifting down, hearing his heart and feeling the snow soaking through his knees only at the very last.

He described these last moments of a man's life for Lucy, and she hugged him at last, her natural good-heartedness and genuine filial love overcoming her embarrassment, her practicality, her nihilism, and said, "Oh Daddy, Daddy, Daddy. Don't worry. Better times are ahead. I know they are. The best is yet to come."

Neither father nor daughter believed it, and Lucy even wondered if she had slipped into a cheap irony or cheap sentimentalism by saying it—but that it had been said was remarkable. This too father and daughter understood: that though "better times" were not ahead, that "the best" would never, could never, come, one of them had spoken of such a wish, and the other had listened.

for Paul Wellstone

narrow road
to the deep north

I am walking down a narrow hallway. A phone rings. I come to an open door at the end of a hallway. The phone rings again. I stand at the threshold, convinced, as I often am, that the room I am poised to enter is, for a reason or reasons unknown or unclear to me, a room I should not enter. My mother appears. She glances at me in a distracted, ready to answer the phone way, then answers the phone. The house shifts slightly in the hot August wind.

My mother's face changes. She is recovering from surgery, so my first thought is that the wound is hurting, but then she says the name of my aunt, her sister, her only sister, Nada, gone now, too—a strange name perhaps for Hispanophones, but she was christened so by Ted and Clara Nestergard, who spoke only English and Norwegian, and however strange her name might be, it is appropriate to this ominous and attenuated moment. My mother says "Nada" once, twice, three times. My aunt and uncle are due in town, coming *up for a visit from Jackson, in southwestern Minnesota, where they farm a great many acres of corn and soybeans. When they return from this visit, the purpose of which is to cheer my mother, preparations for the harvest will begin.*

But here is the news: my uncle will not participate in this harvest. He has been shot. He is dead.

I have told this story a number of times. The reaction is almost always disbelief. Because I appear to be telling the truth, listeners want to believe me, but for reasons I do not fully understand—perhaps they do not either—they want not to believe me, too. Murder in Lake Wobegon? There can be no murder in Lake Wobegon; it is not possible. Anything that disturbing must be absorbed by sly humor and transformed into pleasant melancholy, the deeper pools of which are fenced off by simple common sense. One cannot even tell the story of a murder there: the words fly up from the teller's mouth as if caught in a tornado.

Which is not the worst way to live, but it is a narrow discipline and tends to make a certain sort of person feel unwelcome: me, for instance, at least in the way I saw myself then, a tiny male figure, neither man nor boy, on his back in a vast and neglected meadow of foxtail barley and timothy, under a boiling, luminous silver-and-green sky, telling a story that can be heard only as a roaring, seen only as a black cloud funneling from his mouth.

I told the story to a psychiatrist once. I was being bad in ways I do not want to recall, was depressed, had been identified as a candidate for a course in grief management and spiritual renewal—and, more importantly, had begun to see the blackness of the whirlwind as composed of equal parts self-indulgence (fear of my own sudden death, fear of my own sudden murderousness) and shame over the uses to which I was putting or knew I would soon put the story. I told the story sensationally, for its shock value; I told it so that people might feel as sorry for me as I did for myself, told it so that I might be seen as having heroically withstood horror, told it knowing I would write about it and, while the rest of my family simply grieved, profit from it. As Barry Hannah's narrator says in the story "Carriba": "Murder is not interesting, friends. Murder is vomit. You may attach a story to it but you are already dishonest to the faces of the dead. . . . I knew I had no place arranging this misery into entertainment, a little *Hamlet* for busybodies and ghouls. . . . My whole professional life reared up in my mind. I was a hag and a parasite. I was to be grave and eloquent over their story. . . . They were to get nothing. I was to get fame and good bucks, provided I was interesting. A great sick came on me."

Such was the tenor of my conversation with the psychiatrist. His response was remarkable. I realized only after I had fled his office that he had simply chosen not to believe me. I gave him the murder in précis, with a suggestion of the emotional discord I claimed to be experiencing, and he said, "That's interesting." I waited a good long while for him to continue. He was a kind of Kilroy behind his desk, getting smaller and smaller by the second. Just when he was about to vanish entirely, he said, "I make a special study of stories like the one you've just told me, but I don't recall reading or hearing about this one. Where did you say it happened? And when? I'd like to check the papers. Your uncle's name is . . .?"

I said that his name had been, when he was alive, Art Storm. It struck us both, I think, as sounding made up, the name of a character in a bad novel (if you punch up *art storm* on the LexisNexis newspaper searching service, you get thirty stories on Robert Mapplethorpe and one on my uncle), so I said, "Arthur William Storm Jr." I then described *where* pretty convincingly but was shaky on *when*, which bolstered, I guess, my inquisitor's sense that I was making it up, in a play, I guess, for sympathy. He wrote a prescription for Prozac and sent me on my way.

That was the last time we chatted. Now that I have gotten my facts straight, I want to share them. But I find I cannot recall the name of this psychiatrist, nor when I saw him, nor, precisely, where. The building was located in a downtown Saint Paul backwater; the program was part of that city's social service safety net; and the decor of the waiting room was dominated by fiery orange shag carpeting and dark imitation-wood paneling. My fellow clients either spoke in harsh whispers to themselves ("Not now, you fool, not here!"), turned in very small circles before the magazine rack—which had dizzied and deflected me, too—or stared, stonily or stonedly, into midair. They were both a fright and a comfort to me. Then there was the doctor—elusive, peeping. I took the Prozac for a month; it, too, was both a fright and a comfort. I imagined I felt clear-minded, but predatory. I felt as if the number of rods in my retinas—those receptors responsive to faint light—

had multiplied rather demonically. I could see in the dark and had lots of energy for the hunt but missed both the peace of deepening twilight and the nervous dread of a sleepless dawn. I failed to make my next appointment, failed to have the prescription refilled, failed to balance my chemicals.

A violent act in a violent culture: what of it? Violence can be both fun and rewarding, if you watch the right movies. And I do not mean only those on television or in theaters; I mean the ones we film day after weary day, loops of resentment and frustration and greed and fear and ignorance in which we get the last word, beat senseless those who have annoyed us, and sometimes even kill them, if the annoyance is grievously deep and can be shown to be the cause of a chronic social ill.

Arnold and Sly and Clint simply make entertainingly explicit the features and character of the man many of us daydream about being: a good man—that is, one who knows how to fight but appears to be reluctant to do so, one who is cool under psychological and moral pressure but can explode like a volcano when he needs to, a man not prone to doubt or confusion, a man of deeds not words, a man of action who can gather and manage the collective rage of the savagely annoyed and perfectly righteous people who have defined and approved his goodness, a man who can marshal the virtues and skills his employers say are pertinent and conducive to good public relations. I am talking about a man who can dodge bullets. What better man could we possibly hope for! A man who can see it coming, who can turn aside just in time, engage bad violence with good violence, use the flabby weight of the enemy's badness judolike against him and hurl him into the never-never land of soulless, heartless, mindless evil-doers, a man who can perform the Alchemy of the Good Man: make the lead of superior violence into the moral gold of justice. Above all, I am dreaming about a man who can *remain alive and in control, no matter what, forever.*

My uncle's murderer, a Green Beret from what is always termed the "tough" Eighty-second Airborne, honorably discharged after the invasion of Grenada—in which he saw action of an undisclosed sort—and sophomore English major at Iowa State in Ames, knew all about this massive fraud. "Thank you," his suicide letter read, "for keeping me alive so long." The hero, hoodwinked and helpless. "Thank you for keeping me alive so long." He was twenty-four.

I turned eighteen in 1974 and thus was spared the Vietnam that had troubled me so. Neither sincerely "born again" in Jesus Christ (I did walk down the aisle in answer to that call but really only to get the autograph of a Minnesota Twins pitcher—either Jim Kaat or Al Worthington, I cannot remember which now) nor apostate, I sometimes felt a Lutheran call to be obedient to the prince, to serve my country, and sometimes felt a Christian pacifism welling up in me. But I was also a fan of Heroic Violence. I even had a specialty: I was something, I fancied, of an after-dinner speaker, a guy who could mouth off while trading blows with pinheads.

For instance, the episode that precipitated me into the lair of the shrinking Kilroy: I fought a man on a highway. He had rammed my car from behind, enraged by the way I had gotten in line ahead of him, or "merged," if you will. My first thought was to get his license plate number, and I tried to read it in the rearview mirror—difficult even if he had not been hanging on my bumper. Then I decided I would get behind him. He took the next exit, but I was in a rather taut-handling little German thing and whipped in after him. Still, my only conscious desire was to get his number. Which I got, and began to calm down. But then we came to a red light. I pulled up behind him and then thought, *I cannot pretend this has not happened. I will seek an explanation.* So we tumbled out of our jars of formaldehyde, this sales rep and I, and before I knew what hit me, he hit me. "Is that the best you can do, Chumley?" I demanded to know, but before he could answer, I saw the famous red haze. I began to choke him with one hand, forcing him back to his car and wedging him between the open door and the frame. His arms snugly pinned, his face darkening, I drew back my free fist, in hopes of pounding his insolent face all bloody and askew. But I came to my senses and saw only the natural colors of a cloudy spring day in Minnesota. I released the man's throat and stepped back. I was about to lecture him, but he came flying out at me and landed a good one right in my mouth. The light had changed, and traffic was approaching. I grabbed hold of him and threw him directly in the path of a big orange utilities maintenance truck.

The driver of the truck managed to avoid running over and killing my fallen foe, but the feeling that he had almost not, that the sales rep was dead and that I was responsible—that has stayed with me. It is a perplexing feeling, not so much because it is not true, or because I am filled with shame, but because it is a *good* feeling.

It was one of the first times I had acted on an angry feeling, rather than stewing in my own bitter juices. Getting out of the car, approaching the other—right up to that moment when I started smashing my fists against his window—I was calm. I felt I was "in the right" and was merely going to "redress the wrong" that had been done to me; I was going to be forthright and reasonable. I had already noted the license plate number and was planning on only an assertion of righteousness, acceptance of which on the part of the sales rep would have short-circuited my decision to tell on him, as talking to the cops has always been the last thing I want to do. But the next thing I knew, he was sprawled on the road and a huge truck was describing a screeching salient around him.

I acknowledged, privately, the shamefulness of my actions, noted the "mistakes in judgment," and worked out the causes and effects, but I could not help but interpret it positively. I had appealed to no authority, handed off no responsibility, called out to no one for help or confirmation of what I believed was right and what I believed was wrong. This all seemed perfectly proper to me, even heroic. I had had a bone to pick with an asshole and had nearly killed him. I had understood, in a flash of violently heroic insight, that he was a bad guy, and I was a good guy, and neither of us was going to brook recourse to armed bureaucrats. And I nearly killed him.

What if he had had a gun?

What if I had had a gun?

I had wanted one for a long time. I knew some fellows who owned guns, and I liked them. I went to sporting goods stores and priced them, listened to salesmen describe them, picked them up and hefted them. I began saving money toward the purchase of one.

Television, computer, automobile, handgun: they were all the same to me, tools of American cultural welfare. When they were managed properly, nobody died. My adversaries would be only persuaded—just as they would be by the rigors of any other religion—and corrected.

My uncle's killer did have a gun, a Ruger Security Six (a .357 Magnum revolver, serial number 156-52069) loaded with Peters .38 Special copper-jacketed hollow-points. It was his father's gun, but having been a commando, he was no stranger to sidearms. I do not know if he killed anybody in Grenada, but I do know that he was said to have "come back changed" and that he had tried to kill himself once before. "The last time he attempted suicide he went to Missouri," his father was quoted as saying in an Iowa newspaper. "There is no doubt in my mind he went to Minnesota to commit suicide." The implication is that he could not, for some reason, bring himself to do the deed in Iowa, his home state—an inability I found curious. Were I planning to do myself in, I would most certainly get the hell out of California, which I have designated as the last place I want to die, and go home. But home, of course, is precisely where they keep you alive so long.

The next question is, why Minnesota? "It's strange," said Eric Hagen's mother, "but if you follow Highway 169 from here" ("here" being the towns of Ogden and Perry in central Iowa), "Jackson is almost straight north." Put a ruler on the map, and fill the tank with gas. When you run out, you kill yourself.

Jackson is about fifteen miles north of the Iowa border and seventy east of South Dakota: *coteau des prairies*, the first step up of the great high plains from the Mississippi valley toward the Rockies—the "true prairie" as it was sometimes called, the tallgrass prairie, grass as high as a horse's back and occasionally even higher, up to twelve feet. It is often described as oceanic, a vast swelling sea into which de-spairing pioneer women cast themselves and drowned. But of that ocean nothing remains, as if ten million years have elapsed from the time my great-grandparents appeared on its shore—geologic time, time enough for an ocean to van-ish, exposing a bed infamously flat, across which, in pesti-cide dispersal grids, immense machines move.

For several years after his father's death, my cousin, who farmed in partnership with him (and who found him on the porch), would sit high atop one of those machines in a little air-conditioned cube and listen to self-help tapes while he plowed or sowed or cultivated or harvested. Once in a while he would suffer what they call a false heart attack (which seems as true as the other kind to me). He would be-come suddenly overwhelmed by panic, feeling that his loss, his terror, was not in the past but was steady and continual and happening *right now*, and he would be rushed off to the hospital, where, after a while, the present would expand enough to give his heart, again, the space to beat.

The Des Moines River runs roughly north and south through the country, originating about forty miles to the northwest and emptying into the Mississippi at Keokuk, Iowa. The land for no more than a mile on either bank of the river is folded into hills, giving some parts of town a little elevation and a view, and altering the character of some of the farms along the river: basically, more livestock, less corn.

It was on one of these river farms that my aunt and my mother grew up and that I was born. When I think of farms, this one, and the one on which my father was born and raised (in northeastern Iowa), are the ones I think of: hill farms, polyculture, cattle, hogs, chickens, corn and wheat and alfalfa and sorghum, norghum and flax and beans, wagons and tractors tipping over on steep hillsides—"Just roll with it," my grandfather instructed my mother. There was no running water on the farm, no indoor plumbing. There were bedpans and buckets and pitchers and basins, an outhouse and a well. My mother carried water from this well every day of her life until she left for college. My life on the farm lasted only a month, but what a month! From there it was on to the unspeakable luxuries of Minneapolis: running water, central heating (the farmhouse had a single big woodstove, with a grate in the ceiling to heat the upstairs bedrooms), refrigerators, toasters—luxury upon luxury, to the point where I now do not think twice about jetting to Europe or filling a large plastic bag every week with trash.

Rural America was pretty well electrified by the time my mother was born, which meant, for her, two or three lightbulbs and a radio. There was also a telephone. My mother speaks of her childhood as a kind of idyll of clean and happy poverty—and the orange and the pencil that she got as Christmas gifts, the wood she chopped and the water she carried, do indeed seem integral to paradise. I grew up in the suburbs but can hardly bear to drive through them now. I do not even like reading novels set in the suburbs. My father, who left farm life eagerly at eighteen, saw, with his BBA and CPA diplomas, his income rise sharply the first eighteen years of my life, allowing him to present me with a profoundly different world upon graduation from high school than the one he and my mother had known. My brother and I had already been to California, to Florida (and if I now know a more desperate and corrupt Miami, I will never forget the way the palm trees rattled that first night in the hot, muggy wind), to Jamaica and the Bahamas! I had fished for, and caught, a barracuda. I had already known the impatience Liz Taylor was said to have known in the Joan Rivers joke about slow microwave ovens. I had already experienced the wave of hatred a motorist whose skills I judged to be subpar could excite. There was more money. Our standard of living was very high. You may have heard about this; sociologists and investment fund managers alike have been advertising the phenomenon for years: *rising expectations.*

I think rising expectations are what killed my uncle, actually. How, I cannot say, but I began to think of the .38 Special hollow-points emerging in the bright smoke of the muzzle flash as merely the exploding fragments of the grotesquely ignorant and self-righteous sense of expectation and entitlement that—I began to think—characterized American culture.

I knew nothing of the killer. I knew he felt strongly enough about what he had done to kill himself ("Justice will be done by me," wrote the hero), but what I wanted desperately to understand was how, step by step, he had come to my uncle's farmhouse porch and shot him in the head. This is perhaps the way in which the story became a black whirlwind: uneven breathing in which inquiry became panic slowly rotating clockwise around a void, the void slowly sinking from brain to heart. The killer disappeared. I looked to his country and lo, it was murderous. Each inhalation took in more and more of the cultural atmosphere, each exhalation grew blacker and blacker. Everything about the United States seemed designed to encourage or induce murder: capitalism, technology, the law itself—all nothing more than oppressive religions. I repudiated them, just as I had Christianity and the Lutheran Church that has aided—not frightened—and comforted many of the people closest to me, my mother and my father particularly, whose devotion is genuine and whose freethinking returns them again and again to the bosom of the Savior. And as I went about perfecting the terrible beauty of the black tale—the writer of fiction assuming the pompous posture of truth-teller and coming more completely undone by the duplicity of it than he would have had he simply told lies—the little farmhouse on the prairie came to seem a psychic refuge. By the time I began to think seriously about the place, it had been abandoned for decades. I dreamed of inhabiting it like a character in a Beckett story, or like a Timon of the Great Plains, spitting and howling malediction.

It was not just that my uncle had been murdered, but that my uncle had been murdered *and* I could not make a living. My gifts were being rejected or ignored. My wife had left me once already and was drifting toward a second departure, and I felt sorry for myself: *nasty country, run by knaves for fools, or vice versa, I do not know which.* I closed my ears to the drip and hiss of agrochemicals, to the firm, quiet phrasings of agribusiness executives, and told myself that if I were not the lazy man of letters that— at best—I am, I would be working in a field somewhere, walking neat rows of beans like my grandfathers did. I walked around the farmhouse in my mind, saw the fireflies in the twilight, heard the grossly articulate speech of cattle and hogs—the grunt, the bellow, the squeal, the moan—and the black tale became a murmur and a plume of cigar smoke. Then, in that fairyland of peace and sociologically verifiable contentment, the phone would ring. The farmhouse disappears as suddenly and violently as if a nuclear wind had blasted it. I can see it up there in the tornado swirling down upon me, just like Dorothy's house in Kansas.

The violent act in a violent culture: every one of us is familiar with the ethos of murder. As Freud pointed out, where there is a grave taboo there must also be a powerful desire. The most popular question in the story of my uncle's killing quickly centered on the randomness of it: why would a Green Beret turned English major quit his job as a hired hand on a farm, drive one hundred and sixty-eight miles north, choose a farm out of the blue (the green, rather, a million acres of it), and shoot to death the first man he saw there?

It sounds like a joke: to get to the other side?

"We felt, I guess, all along that this looked like a random deal," Jackson County sheriff Pete Eggiman said at the time. The random deal of the rising expectation: the quintessence of our time and place. Randomness is all the rage, because cause and effect degenerate so quickly into name-calling and scapegoating. But insofar as randomness is a special effect or a magazine cover or a business fad, it is a useless idea, a fraudulent one, a dead end—because, after all the cool graphics and inspirational speeches, it is about precisely what it says it is not: control and manipulation. I used to write videoscripts for business seminars and was amazed to see so many people, day after day, equate *excellence* and *chaos* and *huge profits*. Mid- and upper-level managers taking a day or three off at a convention have a very different understanding of chaos than the guy who appears one fine morning on the loading dock, armed to the teeth and "disgruntled": *I want my job back, I want to feel needed, I know I'm weird, I know I lack people skills, but I am a human being anyway, after all, oh it's too late, it's too fucking late, I've killed someone.* Chaos cannot be measured along a spectrum: there are six billion varieties of chaos alone, and the only taxonomy of importance concerns the ways in which these forms disguise and display their essence, the celestial matter at the bottom of the deep well (this is a line from Neruda to which I came via an epigraph in a book by Gina Berriault) into which artists are forever falling.

I am a novelist (proud to say so, and equally proud to admit that only one-tenth of one novel has seen the light of a bookstore) and operate under the belief that novels and people are ideally suited to each other. Reading a novel is all about the immersion of oneself in the comfortingly familiar incomprehensibility of life and living, in observant incomprehension, in the disorder and beauty of the houses that languages and minds build, in the disordered architecture of language itself. And of all the thoughts I have had of the murdering soldier and his short life, the most compelling is that he was a frustrated writer, that if he had so much as been able to begin to think about a novel of the invasion of Grenada, about a Green Beret who had "never wanted to be strong" (I am quoting his suicide letter again), all would have been well. He would have returned to Ames and Iowa State, continued to read, study literature, write. My uncle would still be farming. His friends would never have had to say things to reporters like, "He was gentle and affable, the nicest guy you could hope to meet." My aunt too, I believe, would still be alive (only in my mind did she die of causes related to my uncle's death; everyone else chalks it up to the tumor on her colon that was to be removed—prognosis for recovery, excellent—and the sudden heart attack—"sudden" in that she was not in any of the risk categories and was only sixty-four), and my mother would not feel quite so lonely, would not wake up every morning to memories of her sister, would not feel the need to wear my aunt's sweater, trying to reconstruct the warmth of her hug. I would be hard at work on an unpublishable novel, not cashing in on private grief and the public taste for mayhem, or maybe reviewing Eric Charles Hagen's novel, listening to him on a panel with Tim O'Brien and David Rabe, though he was not that good a writer; although, on the other hand, the only work of his I have read was written at a time of profound emotional distress, and he had really only just begun.

Why? For what? *Everyone has tried to help. I love mom and dad and Sandy and Mike and Jer and Julie and Tami—all those that tried their best. But I saw this coming in a walking dream, seems like years ago. I have to be so much alone, though I love the animals. I realize now I won't leave this town. I'm not going anywhere.*

Thank you for keeping me alive so long. There were beautiful times. I only wish I could come back.

I'm no criminal, just scared and falling.

Directed inward or outward—pain is still pain.

Sandy—I wish I could meet you again. Stay strong, your strength held me together for so long, I love you forever.

Not only couldn't I change the world, I couldn't even keep it still. There is such a surcharge of violence in me that is not safely directed at anything in this spectacular mystery of a world, though the violence may die, I will not survive as a piece of dust, a fallen leaf, tranquil, unawake, forever a part of this world, forever more at peace. No one should blame themselves for what I have done save me, and justice will be done by me.

I never wanted to be strong.

It is strange that the future can be foreseen, but not averted.

I am allergic to love, a fatal allergy, and in the end I have discovered courage, it is a calm (my first) and it is facing the world
face to face, and only seeing the mirror.

Finis
end of game
no more
will I quench this thirst
the drink is too ugly
the love lost
is too great
these are terrible times
sometimes
we danced
we laughed
those memories
I bring to the wind
the lightning storms
were beautiful
on the front porch
and the purrs and
wagging tail
knowing that then
I was home
I miss you
I miss the simple sanity

But those frames cannot die.
I'm not sure what I have done but I have a horrible feeling, win
the battle to lose the war.

I wish I could explain

I wish there were words to express the love I never showed

I'm hearing voices, like, the whispers of last fall but stronger, all too clear

I am barely here.

The letter was written sometime in the late afternoon or evening of Friday, August 21, 1987, after the death of my uncle, in a room at the Danish Inn Motel in Tyler, Minnesota, a town a little less than a hundred miles northwest of Jackson. The motel was not open for business, but the owner sometimes rented rooms anyway. Hagen paid for his room with a fifty-dollar bill, which turned out to be quite important in knowing who killed my uncle. Once he had rented the room, he went for a walk. Passing Mrs. Bruce Meyer, he noted her pregnant condition and greeted her. "You're pregnant," he said, smiling and friendly. "You could probably use some money." He tried to give her two fifty-dollar bills, which she declined to accept. Hagen carefully placed the bills on the sidewalk, weighting them with a chip of concrete. This was about 9:30 P.M., right around the time I had gone to my friend's house with the idea of borrowing one of his hunting rifles, thinking, *sooner or later I'll be close enough to "this guy" (Hagen), and I'll kill him.* By eleven o'clock my "murderous rage" had passed, and Hagen had written his letter, crawled into bed, drawn up the covers, and killed himself.

"We knew Jackson was missing four fifty-dollar bills," the Lincoln County sheriff said, illuminating the foundation of what we mean when we talk about closure. There was also "bloodstained clothing in the room not related to the suicide." The state Bureau of Criminal Apprehension ran ballistics and blood tests, checked Hagen's fingertips, and found they matched prints on a red disposable lighter found between the porch (the porch!) of my uncle's house and the driveway—it was spotted first by my cousin, who, according to deputy Leonard Rowe, shouted *"Watch out for that lighter!"* as if it were an exploded bomb.

And that was that. Special agent Dennis Sigafoos put it this way in Item Seven of his "Report of Investigation": "The homicide of Arthur William Storm, Jr., has been cleared. The perpetrator of the crime Eric Charles Hagen committed suicide ending this investigation."

Once upon a time, a young man who had been working on a farm in Iowa took his father's car—a white Volkswagen with a black tail fin—and his father's gun and drove north for three hours. A few miles west of the town of Jackson, Minnesota, he saw a remote and prosperous-looking farm. He went to the door of the farmhouse. The farmer who lived there was in the kitchen making lunch. He heard a noise on his front porch and went to see who or what it could be. No one knows if words passed between the two men when they met. Some people believe that a struggle ensued, for life or death, for life and death, but a man who professed to know said that the few minor bruises he found on the two bodies did not indicate any such thing. Silently or not, struggling or not, the younger man shot the farmer four times, twice in the head and twice in the upper torso. There was a large and bloody hole in the farmer's back, and smaller bloody holes in the back of his head, the hair of which was well known for its tendency to rooster-tail. When the sheriff's deputy arrived, he noted that "it was real obvious the party had expired." An investigation revealed the absence of four fifty-dollar bills from the farmer's billfold, money he had just taken that morning at a coffee shop in town as a down payment for a truck he was selling. A cry went up that a vagrant, a drifter, a madman had appeared, had robbed and murdered, had fled, and was at large. But the truth was that by the time most people heard the story, the killer was dead.

Fifteen hundred people filed past the open casket at the wake. The farmer's nephew, at the end of the line, was seen to thump his uncle's hollow chest and cry out. At the funeral the next day, the church was filled with the sound of people sobbing loudly, people who made a point of being cheerful and strong in the face of disaster or misery or sorrow—or at least strong, or at least stone-faced and dry-eyed.

After the service, in the basement of the church where mourners ate plate after plate of cold cuts and hot dishes, roll after buttered roll, slice of ham after slice of ham, news that a young man who had killed himself in a town to the north had been "positively linked" to the murder of the farmer made its way through the crowd. Each person looked into the eyes of the person nearest, then quickly at another and another, saw tears filling those eyes and spilling from them in stern, exhausted relief, felt the force of a hundred spines burning like fuses, shook hands all around to keep those hands from trembling, and smiled, then looked away.

The subject of the death penalty sometimes arises when I tell this story. I am opposed to it, and I present myself as a "crime victim." I say, murderous rage flashing whitely, blackly, in my mind, that if the murderer were alive today, I would want to forgive him. To which the obvious reply is that the murderer is not alive. My feeling, however, continues to be that once you get to know someone, it is hard to want to see him dead.

Plus, what is two plus two? It does not add up to a novelist weakening under a load of ominous dread, every day more and more frightened by—simply and frankly—other people. Clearly, the only way out is to find the well of other souls and drink from it.

acknowledgments

Thanks to Gordon Lish and *The Quarterly;* Mark Mirsky and Allan Aycock at *Fiction;* Sharon Friedman; Bill Henderson, Tony Brandt, and Pamela Stewart at Pushcart Prize; Mark Manalang and *Rhapsoidia;* Elise Proulx at Frederick Hill and Bonnie Nadel Agency; Andrew Tonkovich, who published in the *Santa Monica Review* four stories given up for dead and thereby helped save the author's life as well; and Dave Olesen and Tim Latta, who suffered tragedies and pain I have blithely appropriated.

The author gratefully acknowledges the support of the following journals and anthologies, where these stories first appeared, some in slightly different form.

Fiction: "Visigoth"

The Gettysburg Review: "Narrow Road to the Deep North"

A Motel of the Mind (Santa Rosa, Calif.: Philos Press, 2001): "The Flight from California"

Santa Monica Review: "The Volunteer"; "The Barber-Chair"; "The Free Fall"

Rhapsoidia: "The Flyweight"

The Quarterly: "The Bouncers"

about the author

Gary Amdahl was born in Minnesota and now lives in Southern California. Educated at the University of Minnesota and Cornell University, Amdahl has had several plays produced, and has been the recipient of a Jerome Fellowship and a Pushcart Prize. Amdahl's work has appeared in *Santa Monica Review, Fiction, Gettysburg Review, The Quarterly, The Nation,* and *The New York Times Book Review. Visigoth* is his first book. Amdahl has worked as a bookseller, and has reviewed books for publications such as The *New York Times.*

the milkweed
national fiction prize

Milkweed Editions awards the Milkweed National Fiction Prize to works of high literary quality that embody humane values and contribute to cultural understanding. For more information about the Milkweed National Fiction Prize or to order past winners, visit our Web site (www.milkweed.org) or contact Milkweed Editions at (800) 520-6455.

Crossing Bully Creek
Margaret Erhart
(2005)

Ordinary Wolves
Seth Kantner
(2004)

Roofwalker
Susan Power
(2002)

Hell's Bottom, Colorado
Laura Pritchett
(2001)

Falling Dark
Tim Tharp
(1999)

Tivolem
Victor Rangel-Ribeiro
(1998)

The Tree of Red Stars
Tessa Bridal
(1997)

The Empress of One
Faith Sullivan
(1996)

Confidence of the Heart
David Schweidel
(1995)

Montana 1948
Larry Watson
(1993)

Larabi's Ox
Tony Ardizzone
(1992)

Aquaboogie
Susan Straight
(1990)

Blue Taxis
Eileen Drew
(1989)

Ganado Red
Susan Lowell
(1988)

milkweed editions

Founded in 1979, Milkweed Editions is the largest independent, nonprofit literary publisher in the United States. Milkweed publishes with the intention of making a humane impact on society, in the belief that good writing can transform the human heart and spirit. Within this mission, Milkweed publishes in five areas: fiction, nonfiction, poetry, children's literature for middle-grade readers, and the World As Home—books about our relationship with the natural world.

join us

Milkweed depends on the generosity of foundations and individuals like you, in addition to the sales of its books. In an increasingly consolidated and bottom-line-driven publishing world, your support allows us to select and publish books on the basis of their literary quality and the depth of their message. Please visit our Web site (www.milkweed.org) or contact us at (800) 520-6455 to learn more about our donor program.

Interior design and typesetting
by Percolator

Typeset in Zingha

Printed on Rolland Enviro 100 paper
by Friesens Corporation